Sacred Obsession

by Father
Patrick Bascio

Branden Books, Boston

Library of Congress Cataloging-in-Publication Data

Bascio, Patrick, 1927-
  Sacred obsession / by Father Patrick Bascio.
    p. cm.
  ISBN 978-0-8283-2200-3 (pbk. : alk. paper)
  1. Priests--Fiction. 2. Triangles (Interpersonal relations)--
Fiction. 3. Psychological fiction. I. Title.
  PS3602.A845S33 2010
  813'.6--dc22

                2010043047

www.brandenbooks.com
Branden Books
PO Box 812094 Wellesley MA 02482

CHAPTER ONE

Alex had this dream. For years she sat outside Celia's door, knocking, hoping to be let in. She waited, knock after unanswered knock. Then, one day, suddenly but slowly, the door swung open, as by remote control. She walked in, and there Celia was in the center of an empty room, flanked by unadorned walls, sitting naked and alone. As soon as she entered, Celia disappeared. Alex felt silly, really. All those years, all that waiting, all that anticipation, poof; she should have known that beyond that door there was nothing.

Alex rolled over in the morning light. The sun peaked barely over the lower sill, and a light breeze stirred the loose draperies hanging in front of the window. She felt drugged, as she always did when she awoke from that dream; It seemed that she had dreamt the same dream nearly every night for the last month. Celia was foremost in her mind; the first person she thought about when she awoke the last person's face to cross her mind before she fell asleep. Alex groaned and dropped back onto the pillow. Celia was such a fool to tell her all that she did. She thought she was so smart, but Alex knew she was outsmarting her. From the day Celia began to abuse the priest, Alex decided to remove the gloves. She would get no special treatment, no loyalty, nothing. She was the enemy. Alex would not launch a frontal attack; if she followed that strategy, Celia would win. 'Know your enemy.' Alex would deflect her blows, continually smiling at her opponent while preparing the lethal blow. She would keep Celia talking while she readied the knockout punch. For years Alex had taken second place in their social circles, deferring to her, admiring her feline talents, wanting to be like her. But times had changed. The change came to Celia's attention only at the end.

Celia was motivated by her bizarre and, essentially, self-destructive mission against men. She explained the whole theory and practice. "I love being female because I can control sexual events. Men can't do that because they cannot control their very obvious signs of wanting. Men would be far more successful if women could not hide the fact that they want to be wanted. Men look for any sign that might possibly suggest our willingness to engage. We can handle the 'too forward' approach easily, with simply a sign of disdain. The retreat is swift and complete. 'I did not say 'yes.''"

Then comes the power of watching the apologies, the death of quick passion; the humiliation. Women can be cruel experts at the theatrical flourish. Alex would hate to be a man and have to go through all that. But it's ritual, and is at women's disposal anytime they want to use it. The fixed positions are handed down through the centuries. Without ritual nothing can happen. It gives the man a way in, and it gives the woman the accepted pretense that he has convinced her to let him in, against her will. It's all a game.

Alex did not fit in well with the games that were played. It bothered her that she might listen to Celia and become corrupt, or evil. She just wanted a nice and trusting relationship. Celia made her feel dirty. Alex's reaction, over time, was to stay away from men. Then, as happens with many women, not dating became a habit. She began to see herself as a symbol of womanhood that did not need manhood. Most of the time, almost all the time, she took pride in being the poster girl for independent womanhood. She acquired a reputation as an analytical psychologist; men and women, especially women, came to her for counseling.

Then Father Gregory came into her life and everything was turned upside down. She was a technocrat, the best in the business. In contrast, he was profound; he was a poet. From him Alex began to understand life as it really is, at a deeper level. This was supposed to be her specialty, but from his casual remarks she discovered that she knew very little about human nature. What was she to do now? Now that she had discovered how little she really knew about life, about psychology, about human beings, was she to give up her practice? Alex had a reputation. Thousands came to her over the years, some from as far away as Scandinavia. She appeared in Time Magazine. In the real world she had to juggle the stock answers of her trade to keep the front going. She could not shed her image without destroying her career. Secretly, Alex used the knowledge acquired from Gregory to help her clients.

What she was, really, was the poster girl for the mind of Father Gregory Palermo. She did not feel guilty for not coming out and admitting it; but then his advice, passed on through her to her clients, would help many women. That is a dilemma that Alex did not have time to resolve, so she left it to destiny. Only Celia sensed the change in her, but she misinterpreted it, leading to all sorts of problems.

Alex tried, at various times, to explain it all to her. In the end, Celia's obsession for Gregory overrode Alex's sincere attempts to make her see the truth. But, Alex didn't have to worry about that much longer. Heaven and earth shall pass away, but her love for Celia and for Gregory will never pass away. Was she a fake all that time for not exposing her real emotions for Gregory? That's what Celia claimed the last time Alex spoke with her. She was so righteous at that meeting. Righteous? That's a joke, of course. She was a Eucharistic minister at the parish, and here she was plotting to get him in bed simply because he was not trying to; she wanted to fulfill her mission in life to take revenge on her abusive father. This she did by humiliating men; and what greater prize than a priest? Celia was, if you really think about it, a sexual pervert. However, Alex, did know that deep, deep down, in a place where she feared to look, she had a gut feeling that Celia might have been much more honest than she.

At their final meeting, Celia screamed at her, telling her that all this time she never knew Alex. You should have more savvy than that, my dear Celia. Who knows whom? Look, she was a really well-educated woman. She and Alex both studied Freud in the University. They were not totally taken with him, not at all; but to make sure that the University maintained its reputation for integrity and as a locale of learning, it had to teach Freud. Anyhow, Freud taught them a lot. For example, he taught them that most of what they really know and who they really are lies hidden in their subconscious. Celia and Alex were perfect examples of this.

Alex promised her self that before she lay down to sleep, she would begin the story of Celia and Gregory, and herself. Do you think she won't get much done before she falls asleep? Yes, she will get tired later and she will be going to bed, but not to sleep. Alex doesn't sleep anymore; for what, to rest? You've got to be kidding. She's starting a conversation with you that she really does not want to have. She's doing it for you, dear reader, just for you. As she says, not that she wants to, but, when you read all the circumstances you will understand that it is her duty, a historical imperative, from which she dare not shrink. You see, she wants to be saved. No, just to make it clear, she did not say 'survive.' she has survived. What she need is to be saved.

Celia will linger forever in the lives of all she touched with her unlikely magic. She was Alex's best girlfriend and he was the man she loved:

"I'd like to run away from you but if I were to leave you I would die.

I'd like to break the chains you put around me and yet I'll never try."

Oh how blessed is the heavenly creature that hides from us our future, so that torture can be limited to after-the-fact. We search among the ruins of our shattered lives and find but burnt, chard leavings of what once existed, peripheral images forever out of focus. We thought it wiser to choose continuity rather than entropy. What a joke that is. Look at the mess our so—called sacred continuity has made of things, the suffering. Has God blessed us with this suffering so that we liberate others unknown to us, hooded in mysterious images? Are we the collective incarnation of the biblical suffering servant? If that be so, where the hell are the legions of the redeemed, the liberated? Secluded in His cloud of unknowing, He will never tell.

You see, Alex loved Gregory but he paid little attention to her. He gave Celia a lot of attention because he could see she was so pitiful. He was her priest and wanted to help. Of course, she was not totally troublesome. She did flicker on and off, like a smoldering brush fire resting quietly until a passing wind disturbs its peace. Then, watch out! Just when you thought it was extinguished it can send you tongues of fire that burn your flesh. Of course, he did change his mind, but only when it was too late. He did begin to worry that she was unbalanced and could toss both of them into hell, psychologically and physically. But, it took him a very long time to come to that conclusion. Her sexual prowess, her demands, her insatiable desires, kept him where she wanted him - available. She spawned sexual enticement as a queen ant spawns offspring. She had perfected the art of being, at one and the same time, both demure and provocative. She cultivated her sexuality, spending Saturday mornings in bed until noon, lounging around in expensive and enticing dressing gowns and slippers. She spent a good deal of time on the phone talking erotically with the boyfriend of the moment, washing her hair and grooming for the next assignation. Her soft brown eyes and seemingly permanently moistened lips drew special men to her. Even her laugh was special, soft and showing appreciation, and her grin could sometimes be impish. She would often toss a slow-developing smile over her shoulder as she moved away from a group. Whether it was practiced or natural Alex could never ascertain.

Alex noted that the "average" guy never noticed Celia. She was no "beauty," strutting around with worn patches on the backside of her jeans, or standing around with her hands thrust deep into the back pockets of the baggy khaki shorts she often wore. She did have an attractive hint of a dimple on her left cheek, an asymmetrical beauty spot, but nothing else made you pay particular attention to her looks. However, she bowled over intellectuals; she won all her battles without ever firing a shot. Her silence and shyness caught their imagination, probably because they sensed that her still waters ran deep, the secret tug of the world's most desired women. Understated elegance was the key to her attraction. To the unsophisticated man she was the All-American wholesome girl, even very ladylike on formal occasions. To the sophisticated man, she was a prize worth dying for. To the experienced lover, the man who studied women, she was a bundle of unlit passion waiting to be torched. They sensed it in the way she twirled wayward stands of hair; the way she smoothed her skirt where there was no crease, and crossed her legs when there was no need to do so. They knew she smoldered, and each of them wanted to be the waft of wind that fanned her embers to hot flames. She wasn't really interested in power, although it lay uncoiled within her, ready to spring forth at her command. She just wanted to sleep with intelligent and sophisticated men. She found men of power boring, but the intelligentsia? Oh, very, very sexy. "My meat" she would say and she wanted them in her, where they were trapped, forced, though happily, to murmur words of love and passion. They knew how and she loved to lay back and listen. "I give them what they want, my arms wide open as I listen."

Alex watched with envy as she danced her dance of honey-sweet attraction, light and airy steps, intuitively knowing exactly each movement well in advance. She was lost in her contemplation of Celia, transfixed by her center, a distilled reflection of her reality, unable to observe and assess, as did sensual men, the relevance of her less-than-beautiful frame, a body-fact that in her case was peripheral and irrelevant. Her body language, not her body, is what attracted men. Few women can make that statement. How could those men possibly have guessed that humiliation crouched, lurking just beyond the corners of her femininity? They could not and did not. Usually, such stalking, lurking, crouching, is spawned by passion, but, in her case, it was preceded by vengeance. Alex vowed to write about that a bit later. For the moment, she can tell you that she never inquired of her assignations, or the many trophies she metaphorically pinned on her lingerie. But, Celia was eager to tell her all.

CHAPTER TWO

Alex didn't know whether to thank Celia or to curse her for this diary, this ultimate portrait of herself. After all, everything written here – well, almost everything – she had already told her. But, the written word lingers on forever, haunting and causing others to fantasize whenever they trudge through the painful description of how "satisfying he could be, if she succeeded". Alex wanted to be the one he desired, the one he covered with the soft blanket of his magic.

He was a vigorous man whom people found cheerful and contented. His deceptively soft voice reduced his parishioners to the malleable admiration of teenage bobby-soxers. He catalyzed our discovery of an educated understanding of our faith. His deep brown eyes, trimmed with thick lashes, looked out at the world from what seemed to be a permanently tanned face, bronze-in-motion. His love of the sun radiated from his skin.

The first time Alex met him was at the little fenced-in yard located behind the rectory. He didn't hear her as she approached, matting the grass beneath her feet in soft sounds. There was the smell of a freshly ironed shirt, mingled with the faint but appealing scent of a man's cologne. Her psyche fluttered in anticipation of her first meeting alone with him. He stood in the middle of the yard holding an apple in one hand and looking at it, Alex thought, the way an artist would before portraying it on his canvas. In the other hand he playfully swirled a few drops of wine in a glass, alternating his gaze from apple to glass, at intervals. He heard her footfalls. Their eyes met just above the silvered rim of his wine glass. As Alex approached him he downed his drink and poured another, as if to brace himself for whatever it was she had to say.

She was dressed in a simple peach linen suit and wanted him to notice her figure. She didn't know why, but she wanted to steal behind him as he drank his wine, slip her hands around his waist and press herself against his back. In an instant fantasy she wanted to introduce herself to him as a fairy-queen; just a silly bit of fantasy, born not out of reasoned strategy, but rather of whimsy, a female external sign of internal excitement. Alex chided her self for having such sacrilegious thoughts, but they were there. She would love to have acted it all out on the stage of his perceptions, and perhaps she would one day. now, she would hide it within her secret places, riding the swift horse of her imagination across open fields, her hair floating in the turbulent space created by her passing. In her imagination she offered him herself for use on the sacrificial altar of her devotion.

He seemed to look at life from a distance, never intruding into its reality, but taking stock of it, measuring it and trying to somehow experience its existence among us. He didn't want to change the world. He wanted to be an integral part of it, in all its manifestations. Alex noticed this on many occasions. For example, at Sunday Mass, whenever the piano was playing, his eyes roamed over its landscape, fixated both on the fingering of the pianist and the phrasing of the musical sounds. He bent and swayed with the rhythm, his head resting in the crook of his arms. He would often whisper into the microphone things like,

"Only the gods could write such music; only the gods." He seemed to be talking to himself but it stirred the souls of the parishioners. His keen ear for emotional, social and religious nuances stunned them. They had never experienced a priest like this, a philosopher priest with human dimensions many women did not find in the intimacies of their nuptial bed. They, both men and women, were mesmerized by the lilt of his voice and the accent that accompanied it.

The priests they had known were judgmental. He would say, "Be yourself!" The priests they knew spent a fair amount of time talking about money. He never did. Tim Ryan, the fellow in charge of counting the collection, said, "This is the first priest in my memory who never talks about money, and yet we never had so much. We've been rolling in it ever since this guy came here."

His unspoken spoke to all of his parishioners. There lay beneath his surface a mass of him they did not see, but sensed. What, really, is there to see when the unseen is so appealing, just another measurable dimension? Alex leaned forward and ex-tended her hand, her eyes un-controllably riveted on him. "My name is Alex Walker."

His eyes glittered with curiosity as he nodded. "Hi." His smile was tentative, not knowing who she was or why she had come. His eyes squinted into the early afternoon sun blazing behind her. He rubbed his eyes as if about to fall sleep. He offered Alex a lawn chair of chrome and cane and sat next to her, relaxed, spreading his knees, dangling his arms and hands between them. His face softened. His eyes traveled along the edges of her frame, a laser beam cutting out a form from universal flesh. He surprised her by asking, "You are wearing sunglasses. Do you always do that?" He had a way of asking questions that enabled him to give the answer.

"Well, now that you ask, actually I do wear sunglasses very often, but can't really say why. A habit I guess."

He angled his face and smiled, saying, "Maybe you're a very private person. This way, folks can't look into your eyes and read your soul. That gives you a measure of privacy. Everyone needs privacy. No one has a right to our inner soul except a soul mate. There are no lies when we pretend to be someone other than who we are; protection from intrusion is a human right." He paused and Alex absorbed his exquisite unconventional wisdom. "Anyway, I'm happy to meet you. What can I do for you?"

"I just wanted to welcome you to the parish. You certainly have gotten off to a good start." A hummingbird swept by them at that moment and danced along a flower bush nestled against the kitchen window, his beak busily sucking its blossoms. "I guess I'm kind of curious. What brings you here to Boston? The bio they ran in the parish bulletin says you are from New York City. This is a long way from home."

His lips tightened; his eyes narrowed enigmatically. "Home? I've always been a long way from home, if by home you mean a space of my own, where I can build memories in photos and mementos, a space that I can invite others to share with me."

"You mean you've worked in the Missions?"

He eyed her speculatively and then his face broke into a wide, lopsided smile, looking for a moment like a shy teenager. "Oh, I have, but that's not what I mean. I guess what I really mean is that I don't have a home. I just have different places. I'd like to have a home, but to me a home is a place that a woman makes. I don't have a woman so I don't have a home. Women can have a home. They enjoy fixing it up, making it a nest, even if the nest is empty."

What would have appeared to be indelicate phrasing in

another priest suited him. His quiet demeanor masked what one could easily conceive to be a thunderous inner core, tightly and designedly reigned in. Alex felt a nervous catch in her throat and said, "That's interesting. I never thought of it that way. I would have to think about what you just said, but it is thought provoking. I always saw the rectory as a priest's home, but you've added a new dimension."

His long, tapered fingers roamed along the gold necklace that showed through his open shirt. It highlighted his perpetual light olive tan. His eye motion reflected a negative. "No, the rectory, it's just a place to sleep and put my things. I don't even feel that I have a culture sometimes. I'm very Latin, mind you, but somehow that doesn't situate me anyplace either."

Alex was surprised hearing him speak like that, but not unpleasantly. It was like taking a shower after sweating in the garden. Refreshing is the best word she could think of at the moment. He was a real man, not a 'model' clergyman. It was the first time she had ever seen a priest wearing a thick gold necklace, the kind she had seen young, handsome surfers wear on South Beach, in Miami. It quietly said a lot about him, that he was anchored in the community of men. From that moment on, she was totally in his corner.

He was in her heart and somehow in the growing changes her body was experiencing. As she listened to his sermons she discovered more about her body, her mind, and her values. She wanted him to reach out across the pews and touch her, knowing both that she would be healed and that she would respond.

The phone rang and he stood to excuse himself. Alex thought she should leave. "It was nice chatting …"

He cut her off. "Let me get the phone. I'll be right back."

When he did return he stood a few feet from her, his hands slipped into the back pockets of his jeans. "I am so happy you dropped by. I believe I'm going to like this parish very much, and you sound like someone I can count on for support and as a sounding board for parish opinion. I feel strongly that the function of the priest is to lead, but in a communal way, learning from special people how parishioners feel about things."

Alex was about to offer her services, when he stole it from her, "Would you be one of those persons for me?

It could have been any another question and the answer would have been the same: "Yes," she said, in a definitive manner. A slight facial spasm indicated that he knew what she meant and, perhaps, that it pleased him. "We priests come and go but the parishioners remain. I can only lead properly if I know what your goals are. You can help me understand."

She assured him she would. Alex shared a glass of wine with him, and reluctantly bid him goodbye.

The architecture of his personality stood out above their parish landscape it. He had a way of capturing moods, even the mood of a particular weather pattern. One day, as Alex helped him do some filing in the office, he glanced out at the rainy day and said, "Did you notice that when the wind blows in from the north the rain lends a muggy smell to the air?" Another time he said, "There is something about the sun in a place where it rains frequently. Its rays are a molecular shower moving quickly on its way to another place. It dies and moves on to oblivion, never appearing again in exactly the same context." He paused and looked at her as if expecting an answer to his question. "We are like that, are we not? Death introduces us to oblivion, and we must become companions; we can't avoid it. A good reason not to hold on too tightly to what we have and especially to what we think we are; almost all of which we are not."

He was right. She had lived here all her life but never captured the essence of that thought, and certainly never connected it to the concept of death and oblivion. He had a way of musing on the most ordinary, transforming it into the extraordinary, if this makes sense. The ordinary is always profound; it's just that we don't understand this fact. Alex admired his natural talent. He was always thinking and extrapolating his thoughts, sharing them with everyone. His remarks were spontaneous and light, like feathers gaily tumbling on gentle wind gusts, not the lessons of a tired old academic. In the middle of a sermon, he would recite the most poignant words of a popular love song, a logical outcome of his interpretation of the gospel message.

Alex wanted to give her self to him without reserve. She needed him, something she had always feared might happen, depriving her of senses, suspending her intelligence. There was not a bit of hope that he would ever violate his vow of celibacy, so that is not the point. The point is that this is what she wanted; simple as that. Even the hint of such happenings with other men frightened her. She wanted to be overwhelmed, dismantled and dominated. Initially she believed it to be a fantasy that would dissipate in the cold light of reality, but it uncomfortably persisted. Nothing in her life prepared her for the thirst and hunger that swallowed her up in the belly of its intensity. What she had feared, she now ran to for sanctuary. Alex often imagined standing in some isolated spot, her fist resting on the curve between her waist and hip, like a siren, beckoning him to come and slake, come and take. She began to compare her body with Celia's. There was no challenge. He needed to see her. She wanted him to feed her body and she would feed him in return. The woman's body, after all, provides health, happiness and security to our men. Our touch brings them solace and contentment. It is the circus barker's perfect product, the cure-all and elixir of the male ego. The female body creates an ambiance of manliness all of its own, on its own, without trying.

Could any of this be sinful? Well, not really. If you are a Catholic, you know what constitutes a sin. The nuns made sure of that. The matter must be serious, not trivial; you must reflect on what you are about to do for sufficient time; and last of all, your will must fully consent with what you are doing. Full consent? Can a mesmerized person give full consent to the mesmerizer? Yes and no. Yes, if we had perfect control over ourselves. No, if we mean spiritual consent. After all, there is no consent when a tidal wave overwhelms and even crushes us. There is only an overpowering, non-resistible suspension of self-control, pitiable, even if desired.

Shielding Alex from guilt was her claim to the God-given right to love and happiness, a condition morally superior to barrenness. Of course, she had to admit that she was unaware of her life's emptiness until she met him. But she did meet him. Alex admits and acknowledges that, in the end, the meaning of all that occurs between birth and death is swept away by time and our unknown destiny. "We know now, as through a glass darkly; but then, face to face." Then, and only then will she have all the answers. Our recollections are mere preliminary sketches of the finished product.

CHAPTER THREE

The next week was a busy one for Father Gregory. He met with community Hispanic leaders who asked him if he would allow their people to have a Mass of their own in Spanish, a permission they were unable to extract from the previous pastor, whose policy was: "You're living in America now. Speak English." According to Manuel Cespedes, their leader, "When we explained everything to Father Gregory, he simply said, 'I'll fix that.' It was obvious in his face and his expressions that he was the priest we needed in this parish."

Gregory made good on his promise. He walked into the Parish Council meeting the following evening, spread his hands in a questioning gesture and said, "Why is it that the Hispanics are not allowed to have a Mass in Spanish?"
The members of the Council looked at each other without being able to answer. The parish council chairperson stood up and said, "The matter has never come to our attention, but I know I can speak for all here when I say that we would be glad to hear from you on this subject."

He was prepared. He pointed out that there were, in fact, many Hispanics moving into the northern cities of Massachusetts. Of course, he recognized that Andover itself was an enclave within an enclave, affluent, beautiful, away from the mills. The Hispanics worked in the mills. He had with him a file of letters exchanged between the previous priest and the leaders of the local Hispanic community. It was clear that they had requested such a Mass and that he had denied them. The letter that shocked the members the most was the one from the Archbishop in response to community leaders pleading their case for a Spanish Mass. "Father Jim Callahan is a seasoned priest whose judgment over the years I have come to respect very much. I am confident that he made his decision after careful pastoral reflections." Gregory shrugged his shoulders in a disapproval that was shared by each and every member of the Council. Given the now-known fact that Father Callahan had been forced to leave three other assignments because of his attitude toward parishioners (and no one knew this better than the Archbishop), the letter was seen as both dishonest and an insult to their intelligence. Later, they discovered that Callahan was the archbishop's golfing buddy.

That evening the members voted unanimously to allow Spanish Masses at our parish and authorized Gregory to make whatever contacts or arrangements were necessary to accomplish that goal. His persuasive powers lay in the honest and straightforward manner in which he addressed issues, both general and highly sensitive. There are many disparate layers that make up a parish; also there are many conflicting viewpoints, depending on racial, ethnic and even political backgrounds.

Ironically, he was so successful because he opposed and destroyed all the religious mythologies that would have kept him 'in power' and that have kept his parishioners in bondage, a bondage that was shamefully servile. He used to say, "Please help me conquer all the false dreams and assumptions that parishioners have of me." He demythologized negative mythology.

As the meeting came to a close all of the members stood up and gave him a round of applause. They knew that they now had the kind of priest the parish needed; to move along in its pastoral mission of welcoming and enabling everyone in the area to worship with them, regardless of their ethnic background. Until now, the Mission Statement affirming such an intention had been simply that, a statement. Now, it would take flesh, become incarnate.

Alex accompanied Gregory to the parking lot. Perhaps to symbolize what was to come, they exited the building only to walk into a wall of sleet and rain that in the glare of flood-lights appeared as thick snowflakes. Alex walked him to his car, holding her umbrella for his protection. He stood in the rain for a moment watching the storm before sliding his body into the driver's seat. "I want you to thank all the members of the Council for me. I believe that the decisions made this evening are historic for this parish." He pushed the key into the ignition, warmed up the car's engine, and drove off, giving her a big, friendly wave. She knew they would always be close. In the wetness of that rain they were floating toward each other, but how? Alex was determined to find out. She needed the sun's rays to lighten her way in this gathering darkness.

Just as he was exiting the driveway, Celia, also a Council member, dressed in a denim jumper and long-sleeved blouse, arriving late, raced across the parking lot, trying to unleash a wind-battered umbrella. Her usually pale face, now a flushed red, was raw and wet from rain and wind. She was clearly stricken and confused, her mouth set in a determined line of grimness. "Where is he?" she shouted, almost in anger. Despite the water droplets running down her cheeks, she was sensually beautiful with her shoulder-length black hair and big brown eyes.

"Who?" Alex asked.

"Father Gregory, of course."

There was no 'of course' in Alex's mind. Celia had already told her how awful he was. "But, I thought you didn't like him!"

They stared at each other in silence for a moment and then, tightly, "What's that got to do with it?" There was more than a hint of desperation in Celia's voice. Panic had gripped her in its vise. For a woman who was always in control of her environment, this must have been a terrifying experience. She shuddered. It took a moment for Alex's mind to register this 'new,' out-of-control Celia. "Oh." She said, then grimly, "He drove out as you were driving in."

Celia tilted her head and the parking lot lights exposed the fire in her wide, troubled eyes and the moistness of her parted lips. She stiffened her spine, twisted her head unconsciously, turned on her heel and ran back to her car, muttering to herself. Alex watched the car's lights disappear as it hurtled with speed down the street to the highway. The drum pounded rain on the school roof, further dramatizing the scene. It was then Alex realized that her feelings for Gregory had risen to a new level; a level of 'must see him', a level that could cause her to get out of control. She was not certain that her reaction to this was one of anticipation or of fear. She had a lot to lose if she continued to attract him.

Alex drove home quickly, unzipped the wet skirt, pulled it down over her hips and dropped it on the bathroom floor before showering. As she stood beneath the soft warmth of the water spray, soaking her tired body and shampooing her hair, she pondered the complexity of being in love with the same man loved by her best friend. After toweling, she lit a fire in the fireplace, wrapped herself in a light blanket and spread out on her living room couch, imagining holding Gregory in her arms. The crackling, fire-drenched kindling comforted her and ignited the dry logs waiting to be reduced to ashes. It was a dreamy atmosphere, as the firelight flickered on walls and curtains, forming Rorschach-like figures to be interpreted.

Alex spent some time that evening trying to see him through Celia's eyes, to discover what was going on in her troubled mind. If God planned all these events in His overarching control of the Universe, why is it He never apologizes or asks forgiveness for so much suffering?

CHAPTER FOUR

The First Entry

Celia's diary went back three years, but the first entry in reference to the priest is dated Sunday, August 2, 1997.

"The new priest said his first Mass for us today and I, as usual, with the other Eucharistic Ministers, joined him at the altar at Communion time. I quickly realized that he was focused on me, looking at me the way a man does when he wants a woman. I was completely unprepared for such an event and completely unnerved. After Mass, I avoided passing him as he chatted with parishioners. I did notice that he looked in my direction, as if he was about to say something, but he didn't. I concealed my thoughts with a soft smile"

That same evening, Celia called Alex, a distraught voice pouring out at her over the wires. "You won't believe what happened to me today?"

"What?"

"The new priest gave me that 'I'm undressing you in my imagination' look. I swear it."

Alex cautioned, "Perhaps you just imagined it. How long did this go on?"

"Oh, I guess about a minute."

"Oh, my. Well, let's hope it was just a curiosity on his part. Also, remember, he is a man, a male, and simply might have found you attractive. Did you ever think of that?"

"Well, he's a priest; he's not supposed to be finding me attractive. He has a vow to avoid such things."

Alex thought her statement a bit extreme. "Well, he may have a vow not to be with a woman, but he doesn't have a vow not to look at a woman."

The conversation must have had an effect on her because the next day, August 3, there was another entry.

August 3, 1997

"Maybe I am being too harsh on the priest. Maybe I imagined some of it. Actually, I found him sexy, so maybe I'm reading some of my own reaction in his action. I just don't know.

I think I have already spent too much time on this problem. I should go back to my pleasant daydreams, letting them linger in my mind without all this distraction"

Alex knew all about Celia because she used her as a sounding board for everything she thought and everything she did. It was more than just girl talk, because a lot of girl talk never reveals what is really going on, only what the other gal wants you to believe is going on. Celia was up front. She had a bad marriage and had been sleeping around for years, usually with one man at a time, except when she worked at McDonald Douglas Aircraft. One entry referred to an event that took place about two years earlier. It read.

I had two guys today. I've known both of them for a long tim. They fool around with other girls in the plant so I didn't feel guilty about the fact that they were married. Compliments come fast and furious when a guy wants to have me. But, when they already have what they want it can be different. For example, one of the men told me bluntly one day, when his position in the company was threatened by my ability, 'Don't feel complimented by the attention you get. Men will have anything available' Maybe that's true, but it sure is not something a woman wants to hear. I'm going to take my bath and pour myself a good stiff drink."

Whatever Celia later told Alex about the priest she put in the context of her long history. Her righteousness never swayed Alex. What really swayed her was that when she and Gregory first began to chat about Celia he always tried to make her look good, no matter what she said or did. Celia, like all of us, was a mixed bag. At times, she was brutally honest. For example, one day they were having lunch at Carlo's Pizzeria and she said. "You know, no one has ever really loved me. Perhaps no one will ever love me, but I don't know why."

The problem went deeper than that because Alex also knew that she hated her father. He had sexually abused her as a child and was a tyrant in the home. His advances were not exactly accompanied by tenderness. She hated him for abusing her. Alex thought she unconsciously wanted to hurt the priest as a father-figure. Her labyrinth of whining and truncated threats left her cold, even hostile, but she didn't show it. Maybe she should have. Perhaps if Alex had a more enlightened understanding of friendship, the tragedy might have been avoided. Celia had an opportunity to be loved by him but threw it away. How she wished she had been graced with that opportunity! She would have nurtured whatever feelings he had for her and made them flower. Gregory's entry into her life caused recurring images of bridal wear in her dreams.

Sunday, August 9th contains Celia's next entry.

"The priest definitely went out of his way to make eye contact with me today on the altar. He did more than that. When he handed me the ciborium with the sacred hosts, he said, with a big smile, 'You look like a relative of mine.' How could he say that right there on the altar, with the hosts in his hands? It's clear he was making a pass at me. I'm not going to serve on the altar for the next two weeks. This guy is after women and me in particular. He is a disgrace to the priesthood."

Actually, she only stayed away one weekend. The second weekend she was right back on the altar. It was the first time Alex ever saw her with a short skirt. She did not belong to any feminist groups but she did represent in her private life a bizarre interpretation of feminine discontents, one that was amiably suspicious of men. Several of Alex's girlfriends asked her about the skirt after Mass. She turned away from them and muttered, "I won't do that again. I wasn't thinking straight this morning. Had a fight with my husband Jack."

Alex always thought there was more to it than that. But, as always, Gregory defended her. She said, "I was shocked that Celia wore such a short skirt on the altar."

"I didn't notice." That's the way he was and she loved him for it, but she wished it he was defending her; how happy she would have been. His unwillingness to criticize Celia did not go down well with Alex. She wondered if he would have had the same attitude towards her in a similar circumstance. That thought alone showed she was becoming jealous. Later, Alex did not feel so bad about it, when he explained that Italians really didn't like to criticize women unless the family honor or interfering in a marriage was at stake. Then, the criticism could be harsh and banishment from the family was a possibility. She felt like telling him, "If it were not for her, we might have a chance. You would have someone decent to love you and care for you," but of course she didn't. She realized that she was also fantasizing

But he did like Alex. She took encouragement at the smile that lit up his face when he saw her, warming her like the sun. It made her feel soft and cuddly. When she did not see him for any length of time her senses were benumbed. But then, time and hope have always fallen on her like soft rain showers. The sun inevitably followed, so Alex had no reason to believe that things would be different this time, although she was severely tried. Symbolically, she joined her patients in the waiting room, waiting to see herself as she really was.

CHAPTER FIVE

The third entry was on Sunday, August 23rd. It bristled with ambiguity.

"Once again, I noticed that the priest was what I can only describe as ogling me. I intensely dislike him, but his intelligence and wit do attract me. I will keep myself in check believe me. After Mass I did pass by to greet him, but ever so briefly. I thought he was going to hit on me because I waited until everyone else had gone, but he didn't. Maybe he senses that I am on to him."

That Sunday afternoon Celia called Alex to say that Gregory was being very cautious, that she purposely remained behind to give him an opportunity to show his hand but, clever as he must be, he merely said, "Hi". But, unnoticed, Alex stood about twenty feet away from Celia, observing how she approached him with glazed eyes, trying not to appear interested. After his 'Hi', she made a soft sound and turned her head aside quickly, busying herself with pretending to read the parish bulletin. Then, Alex observed, she peeked back at him through slanted eyes. Her body language gave her away. There was a curve to her lips that hinted at sensual interest. Here, right here, was the beginning of her movement toward him.

Her pretense, however, continued. She interpreted his not flirting with her even though no one was around as a fear on his part. "I am on to his cowardice." That was wishful thinking. It was, in fact, his opportunity, if he were looking for one. The reality was that her growing flirtatiousness made a mockery of her pretended disdain. While being critical she was, at the same time, clinging to him like a limpet. If she had been a patient of Alex, she would have diagnosed her as unconsciously compensating for years of failed love. But Alex avoided having best friends become her patients.

Events proved that he was far from trying to hit on Celia. Her own diary proves the point, but she does not retract her earlier statements. Celia never retracts. Alex observed that in her as far back as when they were high school friends. Her usual quiet voice could suddenly take on a nervous, edgy quality when questioned about inconsistencies. She was not the person she pretended to be. What was actually taking place, in Alex's opinion, was that her sexual attraction to him was in some secret way making its way to her heart. That had not happened in previous liaisons, and this is what really bothered Celia. After all, if she fell in love with him she would then need to give herself to him more than sexually. This and this alone Alex believed frightened her to no end. With the other men, she met them, she saw them, and she conquered them, *veni, vidi, vinci*, as Caesar said. He was different. He didn't need her as badly as she had hoped. Immediately she said, "I'm cutting loose," he said, "Fine." That killed her. He was supposed to beg. She yearned for his forbidden touch. The teasing lights in her eyes belied her protests.

Her next entry was on Sunday, September 8th.

"He is still playing games with me. He did not look at me once during the Mass, except to hand me the ciborium. No smile, no comment. He thinks he's cool, but I'll unnerve him eventually. After Mass I waited once again until all had left the church. I pretended I had lost an earring in the pew. I said, 'Father I lost an earring. If someone finds it, will you have the secretary call me?' My hair was swept back. He glanced at my ears and said, very faintly, 'They are both intact, Celia.' He knew he had embarrassed me but did not show any pleasure in it. He is nice that way. He simply walked away, not looking at me and saying, 'Have a nice week.' He won that round, but I will win the next one."

That day her telephone call brimmed with irritation. First of all, her husband was in the house; that always irritated her on the weekends. "My only time off and he has to sit around here, expecting to be waited on. Lazy bastard!" She was sitting on the basement john, clutching and cupping her phone to her ear, while Jack watched TV upstairs. She whispered; Alex could scarcely hear her. She asked why Celia was so irritated, since Gregory apparently, for whatever reason, no longer seemed to be paying any attention to her. "Isn't that what you want?"

"Yes, but I don't think it's real. I think he's hot for me but is too proud to admit it. You know how the clergy are. They don't want to admit they are human."

"But, you don't want him to admit he is human, that he might be attracted to a woman, so what are you complaining about? Sounds like you would admire his self-discipline if he were attracted to you but not if he is not attracted to you. You can't have it both ways."

This remark irritated her. "Oh, you are just defending him. Maybe you like him. Save that analysis for your patients. I don't need analysis."

The reality was that she was finding it utterly impossible to deny the aching need she had to be with him. She was not, as in her previous liaisons, in control. This, and this alone was the root cause of her frustration. As Alex said, friends never become her patients. But, she can think. Right?

Alex yearned for him to stop her for a chat as she greeted him on her way out of Mass but, at that time, he did no more than smile and wish her a "good day". She admired him so much. He spent his life de-structuring the traditional understanding of almost every human experience. He showed her in their conversations that many times "love" is a way of concretizing the need for a sexual partner and fleeing loneliness. He said, "Even the brutalized may prefer brutality to loneliness." As proof of this he pointed to the innumerable wives who remained in a marriage in which they were humiliated and beaten. He believed that love, in the sense that one truly and deliberately sets oneself aside for another, if not rare, is not common either. He pointed to the statistics. More than fifty percent of all marriages in this nation end up in divorce. Anther twenty five percent, he estimated, remained intact for reasons other than love: children, economics, or fear of another failure. That leaves less than twenty five percent of marriages that "were made in heaven." Not exactly a resounding cheer for the so-called sacred compact.

A few days after that sermon Alex passed by the rectory to drop off a package of parish newsletters to be used in the Sunday liturgy. She entered the yard and headed for the back door. There he was, sitting in a rocking chair, his legs stretched out beyond the kitchen door, capturing the sunlight. He was reading an issue of the *New Yorker* magazine. "No magazine in the world like it," he would say. He grabbed a handful of potato chips from a nearby dish, offering Alex some.

She joined him. She was so happy to be near him. She noticed the electric coffee pot on the kitchen table and poured him a cup. Alex brought up the subject of failed marriages. He said that people like to feel that marriage is not a reason for moving away from old friendships, and, to some extent they are right. On the other hand, if a marriage makes you less of a dynamic person, cuts you off from life, then that marriage is in trouble."

He had a way of cutting to the quick on everything.

CHAPTER SIX

September 15th

The next entry was September 15th. It is the first entry in which she begins to deal, however unconsciously, with her true feelings.

"Today, after Mass, I invited Father Gregory to accompany me tomorrow to the Scandinavian village of Hyde Park. I don't know why I did that. It just blurted out. This means I have to find an excuse for not working in the afternoon. Why did I invite him? Maybe I just want to flush out his thinking and really tell him off. I'm not quite sure. He's beginning to confuse me."

She followed up that entry with another phone call. "I talked with the priest today and invited him to lunch in Hyde Park tomorrow. I don't know what the hell possessed me to do that. It was really stupid of me but I can't just call him back now and say 'forget it'"

Alex was forthrightly cynical. "Look, after what you said about him, why in the name of heaven would you be inviting him for lunch in Hyde Park? I'm beginning to think that you are attracted to him in some way!"

"That's ridiculous."

She pulled back. "Well, obviously there is a reason why you want to see him. You should think about that. If it's just to trap him into making a move on you and then raising hell, I sure don't admire that. I think that would be a terrible thing to do. It's not too late to call him back and say that you're unable to free yourself for the afternoon." She really wanted her to call him back, to call it off. She was afraid that this would be the beginning of the end for her, because she was already very much in love with him.

Celia's face drained to paleness. "I'll call him back as soon as Jack leaves to visit his brother."

She did not call him back. That, obviously, was just a ruse to put Alex off. The next day's diary, September 16th, the first of many long entries, relates what happened.

"I picked up Father Gregory today at the rectory. I wore a

black turtleneck set off with real pearls, and a fuzzy loose white sweater. We drove out to Hyde Park. Along the way I asked him, 'Have you ever been in love with a woman?'

He did not blink an eye. 'I am in love with a woman.'

I suddenly felt very jealous. I wanted to slap him. I know it sounds silly. I was furious with myself, but I kept cool. 'But, isn't that against your vows? Isn't that wrong?'

He was not uncomfortable with my questions. 'I can't imagine that falling in love with someone could possibly be wrong. I also would doubt that one could prevent oneself from falling in love. That's something that just happens, like a wind blowing or a sunset spreading its golden hue right across the horizon.'

His honesty dumbfounded me and suddenly I liked him. Or maybe I liked him from the beginning. I'm not sure. 'So, are you in touch with her? Do you see each other?'

'Only in a kind of way.'

'Because she lives far from Andover?'

He paused a bit; then said, 'Actually, I only see her once a year, sometimes twice."

'Then, why don't you see her more frequently? She doesn't love you?'

'Oh, I believe she still loves me, but, you see, she's dead.'

'Oh, I'm sorry.'

He was very calm. 'That's O.K.'

The town's stores were busy offering fashion displays of brightly colored Fall garments. We were standing in front of a Scandinavian jewelry store and his eyes scanned the offerings in the window case. He crossed his legs at the ankle and leaned right against the plate glass window, peering in. His eyes brightened. 'She would like one of those,' he said, pointing to a series of lapel pins. "I know it sounds silly, but every time I visit her grave, I leave something."

Suddenly I admired him so much and I wanted him for myself. I just blurted out, 'Come, let's go in and look at them.'

I don't know why I said that because I did not want him to buy her that pin or any other pin. Guess I wanted to appear magnanimous or something. I suddenly wanted very much for him to admire me, even to want me.

"You see, the invisible is really more visible existentially than the visible."

I didn't understand the meaning of those words intellectually, but in a different kind of way I understood him; like poetry, which says more than a treatise.

After he bought the pin we began to stroll along the main street. The cute shops fascinated him. Suddenly I hopped out in front of him and said. 'Come close, I want to tell you something.' I kissed him flush on the lips.

He looked startled and did not respond in any way, but neither did he withdraw. After we remained frozen for several seconds he lowered his head toward my face and deftly raised my chin with his index finger. I tiptoed and tried to press my lips firmly against his. This time, he quickly moved me away but I know we vibrated together in a tremulous, mutual shudder. Then, a disappointment. I anticipated what I had often received from other men, a hard hungry demand for my body. It did not come. There was just the soft nuzzle of his lips. I wanted his mouth to cover mine. Instead he teased me with his eyes and a warm smile that really told me nothing, that made no statement whatsoever. He ran ahead of me and challenged me to keep up with him. The "challenge" was probably that he wanted to interrupt this movement toward intimacy. He smiled so swiftly that I was uncertain if indeed it was a smile. "I'll race you to the next stop light."

Even at that distance electricity filled the air of my tiny in-the-middle-of-the-street cocoon. He disarmed me with lilting, softly spoken phrases. But I did not know if the disarming was to conquer me or to avoid being conquered by me. I really do not know what he is up to. In fact, perhaps he is not up to anything. We shall see if he can escape my sweet honey. We shall see. But, one thing I know for sure, I want him. If he does not follow up, he will regret doing this to me. I wanted him to say, at the very least, 'That felt good.' Instead, he smiled and said, 'Well, I guess this is a special day of some sort. Let me get you a cup of coffee.'

We sat in Brownie's Café. He pulled his legs in and straightened out along the lines of the upright chair, looking somewhat like an Asian guru. His flannel sport shirt was open at the neck; the hairs of his upper chest wafted by a slight wind. 'We all need to express our humanity. If it can be done without causing damage it is a gift. Celia. It's fun to be with you. I wondered why this day is the way it is.'

'What do you mean?'

He laughed. 'I can't answer that. In fact I don't even know why I asked the question. We really don't know who we are or why we do some things. It all takes place somewhere deep in us, beyond our knowledge, beyond our control.'

He reached out and gently let his thumb rest on my cheekbone. I gazed at him with melted eyes. He wasn't in a hurry to find out how it was that the day was such as it was. Perhaps, like me, he did not want the magic to disappear. We finished our coffee and continued strolling. I moved my hand to his, but he did not take it. He did put one arm around my shoulder, just for one teasing moment. My hormones slammed against their containing walls. I wished in vain for them to settle down to normal. It was as if we had known each other for years. We drove home and talked about the relationship between art and engineering. He had studied art in Boston before entering the priesthood, so, in his own way he was as interested in form and its malleability as was I. He would also have made a good engineer; my guess is that he would have built bridges, because it takes great art as well as great engineering to build a beautiful bridge. Look at the Golden Gate Bridge, a work of suspended art. He had the instinct for my work, if not the practice.

When we arrived at the rectory he did not invite me in to visit, but he did give me a hug before I drove away. I was grateful for any show of affection. I don't think I will be able to sleep tonight, just thinking about all of this. I need to hold on to myself, to stay in control. I have questions to ask him. Can I get through to him? How powerful is the dead girl's pull on him? I need to know."

Well, there it was, all laid out in clear English. She had fallen in love with him. This was the origin of her continual irritation and agitation. She repeated all of this to Alex when she got home. She was back in the basement toilet with her phone, while her husband was watching Monday night football. "He's not the bad guy I thought he was."

Alex wanted her to keep thinking that he was bad. "Celia, don't take too much from a little peck on the cheek. Don't imagine what is not there. You could spoil a nice friendship."

She just wanted to know her thinking, so she could keep abreast of things, so she could plan her own strategy.

Celia quoted her back. "Didn't you say that as a man he could be expected to enjoy things like that if they were simply handed to him?"

"I did say something like that." Alex was glad this was a phone call because in a face-to-face Celia would have read her body language, and sensed how she felt about him. She did eventually know, but then it was too late to make a difference to either of them.

Alex pressed her. "So, how do you feel about him now?"
She gasped, "I need time to think. It all happened so fast."

"Do you think that the reason you invited him to lunch was because deep down you are attracted to him? Maybe you need to think about this. You just fell for him. Right?"

She wanted her to protest that was not the case, but Celia simply said, 'I'll let you know if I ever get this act together. Right now I'm terribly confused."

At this time, except for her discomfort for him, Alex did not even begin to imagine how things would turn out. Their casual meetings became more and more difficult for Alex to handle. She was jealous, yes, she would have to admit that. But, she was also very concerned that no matter how this played out it could be devastating. If Celia just played with him, he might move from innocence to guilt and all the uncontrolled emotions that could follow. Alex would hate her if she caused his life to become complicated. He was inexperienced. He had had a beautiful love as a young man and it could happen that her sweet honey would unbalance him and he would mistake this for what he had way back then, and make an enormous mistake. That was not easy to contemplate.

Isn't it interesting that, in spite of the fact that they see a living, moving face right there in front of them, they cannot read it as accurately as they can a motionless map? Alex thought that was very interesting, like the real things that go on all around us, the ones they never really notice, rarely go beyond appearances.

She has a neighbor. Her name is Sally. Of course, she and Alex chat all the time. "How are your children today? Will it rain? Are you well? Your husband…?" Never a word about what was really happening with her, to her. She now sees how inane all of that was. The fact is, Sally struggled like hell to keep the family together. He husband was one of the guys, not a woman chaser. She sat alone each night, once the children were in bed, reading magazines, any magazine. Fashion, Love, Child Care, Hollywood goings on, House Decorating. You name it. He sat in his den with his buddies, shutting her out, watching his football, basketball, tennis, Nascar, wrestling, a six-pack at his side. Every once in awhile he would open the den door a crack and shout, "How you doing honey? Love ya!" Assurances that do not assure; unconvincing convictions. The ritual, a kaleidoscope of shifting, weaving patterns of aimlessness. How we kill each other! Then, one morning, the Boston Globe, page ten: Sally Maloney Files for Divorce. She made the papers because her father was a famous lawyer and she had been a socialite. Now, Alex still sees Sally by the house and asks her, "How are your children today? Are they well?" There is no husband to ask about, so she asks about the dog.

CHAPTER SEVEN

September 17th

Her next entry, September 17, two days after the Hyde Park trip, shows that she did not waste any time finding out what was really going on in his mind.

"I called Father Gregory today and asked him if I could see him during my lunch hour, 12 noon to 1pm. 'There's a small park about a 5 minute drive from my office. We could meet there.'

He did not hesitate. 'I'll be there, 12 noon sharp.'

I gave him directions. The park was ideally located about three miles east of my plant, a welcomed patch of green that sat amidst warehouses, truck terminals and light assembly plants. As I drove into the park, there he was, leaning against the hood of his car waving at me, a big smile lighting up his face. He made finger motions indicating he would join me in my car, which he did.

His forthrightness of Sunday continued. 'What can I do for you today, Celia?' He just looked at me for about a minute, as if trying to figure out what was going on with me, and said, 'Well, to what do I owe this unexpected but pleasant meeting?' I find that in life we continuously keep looking at each other for clues, trying to figure out what is going on, and never really discovering.

It seems like every time I wanted to ask him something serious, I could never get myself in a calm, cool presence. I usually just nervously blurted out things. 'I want to ask you about the woman you love.'

'Well, I fell in love with her when I was very young. I mean really young; I was a sophomore in High School. It was dreamtime in my life. She expressed her love for me in a thousand different ways. No one since has ever expressed so much love for me. She gave me herself. The emotions were extremely powerful and we both wanted to be one. Isn't that the definition of marriage, two in one flesh?'

'Yes.'

'Well, then, we thought of ourselves as married; in love and married.'

He confused me by the juxtaposition of his sentences, but, as

I've said, in a manner poetic. I asked him, 'What is love?'

'What is love? I suppose what a woman calls love and what a man calls love may not be the same. I mean, it really is the same, but it is explained differently, so differently that there is an appearance that men and women mean something different, but that's an illusion. It's just the ontological, primitive difference of two parts constructed to fit together. Just stop for a moment and think. If the two parts were constructed identically, they could never fit together. So, it's not that the differences are separators. On the contrary, their differences make meshing possible.'

'Differences are both illusions and a necessary reality?'

'Yes.'

'Meaning?'

'First of all, let's look at it from the woman's point of view. A woman, and correctly, draws the conclusion that all men are alike, meaning that all men want intimacy with a woman.'

'Well, isn't that true?'

'Yes and no.'

'Tell me. Explain.'

'Well, there comes a time, if a man is lucky, when he meets a woman for whom there is an immediate and powerful attraction that goes beyond the body, but includes it. He has an intensity about her that is different from emotions he felt for any other woman. He is in love. This happens when men make the distinction between desiring a woman, and desiring only this particular woman. The love doesn't negate the desire; it simply transforms it. The desire is at a different level, or place or intensity. God has something to do with all of this, so it's simply beyond our comprehension. It's marvelous; it's frightening; it has a different kind of intensity, one that's godlike."

He paused and thought a moment. "Oh, I don't know how to explain it. I can just tell you that it is real; you would have to be a male to understand it. Love is stronger in men than in women. Look, who writes most poems? Men or women?'

'Men'

There you are. That's what I mean.'

'The woman's love is not as focused. She has to feed the kittens, cook meals, dress the kids for school, pick them up from games, etc. etc. The man, if the love is special, focuses, adores, idolizes and worships. From that time on he is in love and he wants her, yes, but only her.'

I wondered why I was asking him all these questions. What about all the experience I've had? It was much more than he will ever have. And yet, suddenly it was as if I knew nothing, had learned nothing. Is that possible?'

"I experience such a love and it still resides in me. Certainly! do not see priesthood and love of as mutually exclusive, except for the fact that my love is focused, but on a group instead of a person. That is very tricky.'

'You mean the Church made a mistake?'

'No, not really, I mean not the Church, if you mean by Church bishops and priests and the pope. Not that. It's a mistake that man has made, and when it was made it was made with good intentions, like a priest being totally available to the people. But, it just has not turned out that way. In some ways, the isolation he lives in works entirely in the other direction, make him less available, less human, less understanding of human nature. I'm happy I was in love. I would not want it any other way, and I'm sure if I had a wife I would be a better priest. It's not like blaming anyone or any institution. It's just the way life plays out.'

Celia's diary transfixed Alex. She read all of these conflicting emotions, with alarm and envy because he was confiding in her. The dead girl made him what he became and he no longer had a choice to be anything different. Because it happened to him, that early love, he will always be that, priesthood or no priesthood, alive or dead. He can't be something he is not. If he ever tried he would have destroyed himself. He never destroyed himself. Celia destroyed him. And for that, Alex did what Alex did, and she will never regret it. It was the right thing to do. She knows it may not make any sense, but then life is a mystery and in a mystery there are dark corridors that we never comprehend.

Celia told Alex parts of the conversation she had with him in the park, but not all the details that Alex read in her diary. She was helping him one day in his office, updating the list of those home-bound parishioners who needed visitation by the priest. On the basis of what Celia told her, she was able to maneuver him to talk about the dead girl and his love for her, like how it all happened. She kept looking for a way into his heart. She asked him if he had ever been in love and he told her about his young love, basically what he told Celia, but so much more. He spoke about how it all happened.

'Yes, we first met at a night football game. That's how it all began. Unplanned, no romantic setting, no long discussion; just like that. From that moment on we could never be without each other. To be separated would have been so painful that we would have died. Incredibly, our parents understood that we were inseparable. They pretended they did not see what we were doing. They fell in love with our love. They became starry-eyed watching us. It was unbelievable. I'm not sure but I think they fell in love all over again because of our love."

Alex felt so bad for him. The hurt in his voice hurt her, but she was glad to know that he was not falling in love with Celia. She could not have him because of his priesthood, but Alex wanted to protect him. She was afraid that invincible Celia would destroy him.

A wisp of wind loosened a tendril of her hair, slapping it across her face. He took a moment to lift it up and place it back. She could feel his tenderness. He cast a practiced eye at her, measuring what, she was not sure. He said, "If you need a friend at this time, I am always available." He knew peoples' needs. He read minds, and he was willing to go a step further than most priests and remove the barriers. It was also clear that in moving the barriers he was not providing access to his body. In that sense he played with fire, but he could not see the priesthood in any other way. Alex knew what was going through this mind because he spoke so often of his experience of priests as a young man. "They would just call you into their office and stare at you from the other side of a big desk and it was all so impersonal and at times even frightening." He was determined not to be like that, and he knew full well the dangers involved. He never said anything that ever indicated that he felt he was superior to other males in any way.

They completed the new sick list and he walked her to her car. He did not hug. He just said, 'See you later,' with a nice smile. She got into her car and drove off.

Alex had expected him to say, 'Well, I'll see you again soon", but he did not. And yet, she knew that if she ever wanted to see him he was available. She had hoped that their growing friendship would make him more aggressive, but experienced the emotion that it did not. He remained close but distant. She wondered privately if he found this difficult to do in her case. After all, he knew from the way she acted that he had an invitation to do pretty much what he wanted. He was different. Alex knew that if she had not fallen in love with him, at least part of what happened would never have happened. So, she can't just walk away from all this and start a new life. That is no longer possible.

CHAPTER EIGHT

There was a three-week lapse in her diary, but not in her conversations with Alex. That was an unusually long period of time for her not to communicate with herself. Alex wished she knew what went on because now she hung on every word written by the woman who was courting the man she loved, looking for clues. Celia would always let days pass without calling when something irritated her, even if Alex were not the source. It was clear to her that she was seething with a new reason for anger: He was not pursuing her. She wanted some action. Celia was accustomed to immediate reactions to her siren calls. She kept expecting Gregory to call, but he did not. In frustration she called him and invited him back to the park. They met and that pleased her; she was flexing her groin muscles.

However, she was not prepared for what he said. He told her that he planned to leave Andover in about nine months; the archbishop in Boston wanted to send him to the mission in Peru supported by the archdiocese. Gregory's fluency in Spanish was the key reason. She didn't panic, but she did decide to make her moves in fast forward. She had been willing to take her time, confident that he could not escape. Now, there was a sense of urgency.

Actually, Alex saw it the same way. She needed to step up her own courting. She needed to be bolder. But, in a way, his decision to leave for Peru did level the playing field. It even gave Alex an edge because she was not tied down. She could, and she definitely would, visit him in Peru when he got settled. She would study some Spanish. She was a bit annoyed that he had not told her he planned to leave, but she had to accept the fact that, at this point in time anyway, he had no favorites.

Oh, yes, there was another very big plus in all of this. It was clear from his decision that he did not plan to get involved in a long-term relationship with her. Alex needed to stay calm and, like the sly fox, lie in wait. She knew Celia would not follow him to Peru. She couldn't do that. Alex knew that she would not abandon both her husband and the job that was very important to her. She was proud of her engineering skills. She also prized the extraordinary reputation she had acquired in the community. She was shrewd. She once said, "You might say I lead a double life, but doesn't everyone? I have no intention of allowing the society wolves to chew me up. Never. Always pay close attention to the externals, my dear Alex. Remember to advise your patients." That was the grounding of Alex's hope. She would never leave her home and Jack for Gregory. All she needed to do was be patient.

Alex could see her pulling out all the stops. She spent so much time criticizing Gregory to Alex that, given the nine-month deadline, she would have to eat crow and move quickly on all fronts. Her first step was to admit openly that she had misjudged him in the past. "I realize that I judged him too quickly. I'm not so inflexible as to be stupid. I've made a decision to be very nice to him."

Alex asked her what she meant by 'very nice.' She played the cutie and winked: "Whatever it takes to make him happy."

"Sex?"

"Whatever it takes."

"Where are you going with this?"

"Wherever he thinks he wants to go, but precisely where I know I want to go."

"Marriage?"

"Oh, God, no."

"And if he wants that?"

She smiled an arrogant smile. "I'm like the Mafia. Once I let you in, you can't get out." Then she laughed a most unusual belly laugh (unusual for her because she almost never laughed loudly). Alex felt superior to her because here she was gathering intelligence on the enemy and the enemy handed it to here by the bushel, totally unaware.

Two days later Celia took a positive step. She offered to bring him a few doughnuts (he loved them) at noon. He said he would be happy to meet her at a Dunkin' Donuts, both because she could join him for coffee and it would save her the trip all the way to the rectory during her lunch hour. What she really wanted, of course, was to be alone with him. "It is no problem. I am passing by Dunkin Donuts, so I will pick up a few and bring them to the rectory." She was moving in for the kill. "I bought some new clothes. He's going to get first-class treatment."

What happened at that meeting, she described in her diary entry of Sept 24th.

"Well, I had quite a day with Gregory. I went to the rectory and we started out with a cup of coffee and shared doughnuts. He asked me if I had ever seen the rectory. I said I had not, so he took me through a walking tour, both upstairs and downstairs. I told him I did not see a bedroom that looked like it was being lived in. He said, 'Oh, mine is on the first floor behind the kitchen. I didn't think of bringing you there.'

"Are you afraid of me?" I asked him.

He replied, 'No. It's just that I never bring anyone back there, that's all.'

That, I think anyone would agree, was a provocative sentence, a clever way of bringing up the subject of touching. He doesn't fool me one bit.

I just said, 'Let's see what ghosts we find there.'

He outmaneuvered me. "Another time, Celia, when I have an opportunity to tidy up. You know, my room is a bit messy. I guess, typical male."

I could read him well. He was playing hard to get. He is unaware of my power, but one day I cam going to put it out there full force. He is playing games with me. He wants me but he does not want to lose control. Well, he has another thought coming if he believes that he is going to be in control of this situation. I am an expert. He does not know whom he is fooling with. I put my hands on his shoulder and his chest. I could feel the electricity all around us. His face lit up like a Christmas tree. My legs weakened beneath me. The atmosphere was magic. I never before experienced that kind of sensation. I remember holding on to myself real tight. Everything swirled around me. I was totally absorbed in his personal ambiance. He pulled back once and gazed at me, his eyes hard on me. I could not read his mind. I am sure the air between us was rife with particles of sensual attraction. But he hid his feelings from me. He just simply said, 'Now, let us have those donuts.' He thinks he can outsmart me. He wants me to beg him, but that will never happen. I will put him on his knees. Just watch me. The bastard thinks he is so invulnerable that he can wait for the moment he wants and then take what he wants. But, he has no idea what he is playing around with. He will find out soon.

I stood on my toes and kissed him on the cheek. He pulled away. 'I don't think it's wrong for two people who like each other to be affectionate. We just have to know when to stop.' He said this with a stretched smile, but I didn't think it funny. What a ridiculous statement. We parse paragraphs and sentences, not intimacy. He is so incredibly stupid and naïve and inexperienced. I hate him for that. Who the hell does he think he's fooling around with? I've had men beg just to kiss my foot. I can have anyone I want. I've proved it over and over again. I am femininity.

What bothers me the most is that he moves like no one else has ever had. He moves like a panther, quietly, through the foliage of my existence. The lingering effects of his presence continued throughout the day, and that night I folded myself on the sofa downstairs while Jack watched the news in the living room. I'm falling in love. Damn it, that's one thing I don't want to happen, ever. I'm very uneasy. I've never been in love so I don't know if that's what this is. Many men have tried to outwit me. They have all failed. I do need to control my images if I am to remain strong and fearless, if I am to teach him a lesson. I hate imagining him but having a bit of difficulty controlling it. I will control it; there is no doubt about that. I am much stronger than even I credit myself.

I imagine him staring into space. That's an affected air, and he has it down to perfection. I will give him credit for that. I am the only one who understands that it is a ruse. He does not fool me one tiny iota. And yet, I imagine that pose when I'm driving, working, showering, eating. Not to worry, dear self, I will get that completely and utterly under control. I imagine him praying before church icons. I'm not someone who refuses to give others credit for their talents, not at all. He fools everyone. Even myself, but, you understand, only momentarily. Oh, my God, even the wise can be manipulated, but in my case only fleetingly. After all, I'm human; I'm not really worried. I will dismiss these images like the foolish but controllable fantasies they are. I am, Jack innocently reminded me the other day, forty years of age. Oops! I almost wrote forty years old. I am ageless. But, what if just for fun I had written forty years old. So what? Would that not make me even more remarkable? Of course it would. Don't be jealous enough not to admit it. Don't be petty. I hate pettiness, even in women. We need to be more manly in that regard. Even I will admit that. The important thing for him to know is that I am woman and I know how to strike. He will find out."

As Alex read that entry, she began to realize how vicious Celia was, and how dangerous the situation was for Gregory. She knew that women need to have stealthy ways of defending themselves. Fists are not their answer. But, really, Gregory's assertion that it is OK for people who like each other to embrace and kiss on the cheek is common sense. He understands, and he was only expressing this to her, that as priest he needs be careful with whom he engages in that manner. That's not because it's wrong (my God, all males and females hug and gently kiss if they are close, or were classmates, or know each others' spouses), but simply because of the simplistic perception of priest that people have. Of course, it's the Church that fosters all that nonsense, so it can only blame itself. If the Church were honest, as is Gregory, that skewed perception, that twisted understanding of celibacy, that myopic vision of church would dissipate, disappear into oblivion, as it should. If Alex worked as a psychological consultant on the basis that everyone is perfect, she would be a totally miserable failure. Don't we read in the papers about clerical homosexuality, pedophilia, and stealing from church treasuries? Of course we do. When will those higher ups ever get real, face facts? They speak of the wonders of Christ's incarnation. Why don't they actively encourage such incarnation among their official representatives, among those they claim (and Alex is not doubting it) to be other Christ living among us? They should get a life.

CHAPTER NINE

Celia did not mention the rectory meeting to Alex until later, but she did recall that during that period Celia spoke less about him; she seemed to be backing off. However, Alex knew her too well to get very hopeful. She always, ever since high school, struck like lightning, coming from left field, as they say. She was a very unpredictable person, but also very capable of hiding that fact from her friends. Everyone in the parish, the folks at her job, knew her as a very shy, sweet, steady creature that would not hurt a fly. Alex was her one exception because she was the one person in the whole world Celia confided in, the only person she trusted completely. For that reason, Alex now experience anxiety, she knew too much. That can be dangerous. She was the only person to whom Celia could be vulnerable. Not an enviable position, because she analyzes everything. They simply had a fraught relationship, and fraught relationships can be very intimidating and fearsome. Better never to have known than to have known and be known, and maybe even targeted.

A chain is only as strong as its weakest link. In her chain Alex was that weak link. She was fully aware. Here was a woman with a secret life, a predator of the first order, who made a decision that she wanted to get this priest in bed, whatever the cost. She needed a victory. She had never lost a sexual battle in all of her life, excepting those with her father; that was understandable. He was, after all, a grown man and she was only a child. Even her mother dared not interfere. After him, she was determined never to lose a battle with a man. Alex believed, but was not certain, that beyond revenge and the desire to inflict humiliation, lay something Celia would never admit to herself, and perhaps, to some extent most women do not like to admit. In inciting lust in men she also garnered pleasure. Yes, sexual pleasure, a pleasure only a man can give. It's obvious, but don't we dismiss the idea from our consciousness? I think we do. It's not ladylike. Women are the pleasure givers. Well, we are, of course, but not exclusively. We also receive.

When she began attracting men, and realized that she attracted what many women would consider the best, she would retaliate for what her father did to her. She would humiliate, taunt, tempt, and destroy. In her illusion she is on a search and destroy mission, in search of her father. And now, the biggest prize of all, a talented, well-loved priest who she perceived as screwing around with her head, had to be taught a lesson. It would never occur to her in a million years that she wanted him to pleasure her. That would be an unthinkable thought in the culture of her mind. Of course, Alex knew all of this now because it's all laid out in the diary, albeit in code; but at the time, she could not follow her moves.

Alex recalls that at one point, when she offered him a rare compliment, she asked her, "What do you find so exciting about him?"

"There are so many things. I love his intellect and his modesty. He's not 'the boss'. That shows how much self-confidence he has. I like that in a man. I love the way he walks. When he talks about the world, it's not like the guy who went on a tourist trip and fills you in with every boring detail. He draws philosophical, historical or political lessons. But, if I were to distill all of that and try to give you what he is in a word, I would say 'gesture.' A movement accompanies everything he does, and the movement defines the subject. Incredible. But, remember Alex, I have serious reservations about him. You know, he flirts with me and then runs away. I don't like him for that."

If only Alex had taped those complimentary remarks; she would have played them back for listening later on.

Her discourse was what they call in method acting, mobile. She flicked her words, throwing them out to the listening in swift jabs. Nothing new. In our normal discourse we don't choose words carefully; we simply, without consciousness, call on our memory bank, and the tone we attach to the words is the byproduct of all our experiences. If people listen to us they would know us; unfortunately, they spend their time looking at us.

Her compliments, on reflection, indicated to me that she had entered a new phase in her strategy. If she were planning something big, she might well have decided to throw everyone off guard, even me. Looking back, I see that she did not want to appear as his enemy. That could arouse suspicion should anything happen to him. She was, after all, brilliant. So, on the one hand she praised him; on the other hand, she balanced that with legitimate criticism. He should never have kissed her on the cheek and hugged her privately. He was not wise enough to know that women, under the right circumstances, might interpret signs of affection as more than intended, and even use them later to inflict harm. But then, all men are vulnerable in this way; in that sense he was no exception. He was, after all, a male, and males can be very naïve when it comes to women. That's where they trip up, and it appears this was his problem. He fell on his own sword.

She was correct in her observation, but only up to a point. Alex says that because she was no innocent schoolgirl when she wrote those words. Here was, after all, a virile male, albeit a priest, with whom she not only flirted but to whom she unabashedly made herself available. In Alex's opinion, given all the dynamics of such a situation, one might more reasonably praise Gregory for only kissing on the cheek and giving a couple of hugs, even tight ones. Priests are just men, not gods. Unfortunately, we are a long way from being honest about that, adding to, rather than solving the problem.

Let me not stray too much. The point is that for the first time in her life she had the possibility of being pleasured even as she pleasured. Secretly, in my opinion, she felt she deserved finally to experience and receive that which she gave, even if, in her giving, she had an evil agenda, the destruction of her father. I mean, don't kid yourself; she knew exactly what she was doing. She hated herself for hating her father. She knew she was on the road to self-destruction, but she wanted to blame someone else for it all. Neither did she want to self-destruct alone. That would have been a humiliation. Gregory and I were the most visible and vulnerable targets. If she went down, she had no intention of going down alone. Her sin was the one unforgivable sin, despair.

CHAPTER TEN

Shortly after the incident in the rectory Celia erupted in righteousness. She called Gregory and told him that he had used his authority to take advantage of her. She accused him of being a disgusting priest and person. He should be thrown out of the priesthood for going too far in the rectory, making a sexual situation out of an innocent visit, luring her on sacred ground in order to excite her. She implied that she might report him to the archbishop.

"At work I started thinking about that priest, luring me into the rectory, making me hot for him and taking advantage of me. To humiliate me he first hugs me up, getting a cheap feel in the process, and then, having aroused me, pretends that it would be improper to be intimate in the rectory. What a lousy hypocrite. He hugs me up, kisses me and then piously says, 'We shouldn't go further.' I hate the bastard and I'm going to call and let him know how I feel."

Actually, she called Alex first and detailed her version of the meeting, her voice reeling through the airwaves like cannonballs. She suggested Celia calm down and, for the first time in the many years that she'd known Celia, she abruptly hung up on her.

Gregory called Alex shortly after he received her call. He was devastated. "I didn't lure her; she lured me. She set me up."

Alex asked him if they could meet for lunch. He was real hesitant. After receiving her lurid phone call Alex was sure he was leery of meeting any female. She gently pressed the point, telling him that she had something important to discuss with him. After some hesitation on his part, they agreed to have lunch at the Italian Gardens. Alex had two reasons for this meeting. The first reason, she wanted to make it very clear to him, face-to-face, eyeball to eyeball, that if Celia reported him to the archbishop she would voluntarily visit the archbishop and explain the background to all of this. For Celia, to talk to Gregory so roughly and with threats after she had been throwing herself at him for weeks was more than she could bear.

The second reason, let's face it, is that Celia's latest nonsense would certainly end his relationship with her, leaving open the possibility that he and Alex could develop a measure of closeness, even if it were not sexual. She knew she could not compete with her in that area, though she was willing to try. Who knows how she would develop under his touch?

Meeting Gregory at the Italian Gardens made Alex feel like she was on a date with him. She had always been complimented on her long, shapely legs, so she took full advantage of that and wore a short skirt, something she had not done for about five years. And of course the thought did flit through her mind that she needed to be careful not to begin a round of actions similar to what she was condemning in Celia.

Gregory was guarded in his greeting, not knowing what to expect. Alex made a few silly comments about the parish choir and about one of her dogs. He was very calm, but did not hesitate to get to the reason why we were meeting. "Now, Alex, I know you invited me here so we can have a nice Italian meal, but you indicated that there was something else on the agenda. Tell me."

She surprised herself by not being a bit nervous. His calm directness made her feel instantly at ease. Her first thought was that she should have invited him here long ago. What seemed so difficult turned out to be easy and relaxing. Energy flowed smoothly between them. She addressed the issue. "Celia confided in me the call she made to you, how she ripped you up and down, and called you a bad priest."

He remained calm. "Yes, well perhaps she had good reason to do that. In any case I ignored her belligerence. She might have been having a bad day. Did she tell you about our meeting?"

"Yes, she did."

"I mean, did she tell you what really happened at the meeting?"

"Yes, all the details."

"Well, there you are. Should I not be ashamed of myself? Don't I deserve her anger?"

Alex looked him straight in the eye. "I might have thought that myself, but I knew what she had been planning."

He was a bit startled, "Planning?"

Naiveté, normally so appealing, in him, at this time, exposed him to deadly poisons. She explained, "Just a couple of days prior to your meeting with her she said you seemed to be avoiding her, so she was going to take some positive steps to develop a better relationship with you."

He continued to defend her. "That explains why she chose the rectory for our meeting but I'm afraid, Alex, that it does not explain why I reached out for her and kissed her."

"On the cheek, right?"

"Right."

She pulled out all the stops. "She told me she kissed you on the lips right on Main Street, in Andover. Is that true?"

"Yes, it is."

She wanted to sever the chords that bound him to vulnerability. "That makes her protest about you kissing her on the cheek, if that's what you did, look a bit ridiculous to me." She got a certain sensual feeling just saying this to him, like they were both entering a forbidden but enticing zone.

As usual he made no negative comments. Alex encouraged him to defend himself. Celia could really hurt him with the parishioners and the archbishop. She assured him. "If she reports you to anyone in authority, I will go to that person and explain how she went after you and set you up."

He smiled, "That's a quick way to lose a friend of many years." He loved in so many different ways. His center was all of us.

"I know, but it would be so unjust."

He thought for a moment; then said, "Well, let's see what she does. I do think that what you have just told me would put the incident in a different light, at least for those who are willing to listen. But, a woman crying sexual harassment has a lot in her favor. Don't you think?" Naiveté and reality played point counter point to his personality.

"Yes, I agree, but I'm also a woman and a woman who knows Celia very well. They will listen to me."

He started to put his hand on hers but pulled back. His caution continued. "I thank you. Not many women would step forward like this. You are a brave little lady. If I get any pressure I will call you."

The tender and innocent look on his face deepened her love for him. Cynics tag adult innocence as mythology. How wrong they are. They need to look for it in the right places. Alex decided right there and then that she would do everything possible to protect him. She would continue to play her friend, while attempting to thwart her malicious actions. This way she would know her every move. She would be able to warn him. She was on his side and it made her happy. What was left of their friendship ended when Celia threatening to destroy Gregory.

Alex was so happy to be his guardian angel.

CHAPTER ELEVEN

Alex's happiness was short-lived. He phoned, believing he was giving her joyful news. "Celia just called me to say that she is so ashamed of herself for her uncalled-for behavior, together with the awful threats she made. She's really repentant. I had to call you right away. I knew how pleased you would be, since she's your best friend."

Alex had a different take on her call. To her Celia's 'confession' was but an omen of further deviousness to come." Do you believe her?"

"Well, that's irrelevant. I'm going to stay away from her anyway, for many reasons, not the least of which is that when I'm alone with her I do tend to get foolish and lose my focus. So far, nothing serious has happened, but she is very appealing, so I need to keep a guard on myself in the future, to practice some preventive medicine. If she was capable of making such a big item over a hug and a kiss on the cheek, imagine what would happen if I ever touched her, however slightly and accidentally? My God, there would be hell to pay. That's for certain. She would crucify me."

He was beginning to understand that in order to survive in her world he must strap caution to his loins. Alex blurted out. "Would you like to have sex with her?"

No hesitation. "Theoretically, and if we were both free, who knows, but neither of us is free, so, in that sense, absolutely no, no, no."

"Do you mean that she is stuck in a marriage that is really not a marriage?"

"NO, I do not mean that at all. She could always get an annulment, if the situation is as you say it is. The Church checks into marriages like Celia's. If one of them can prove that they were not suited to each other from the beginning, there is a good chance such a marriage can be annulled?"
"How would you feel about her then?"

He just laughed. "At this point the only thing I can tell you is that I need to keep my distance from her, and not speculate on what ifs. There are three reasons for this. I'm not in love with her, I'm a priest, and she is unbalanced. It would all turn out very badly." After a long pause he said, "Actually, there is another reason, but it is more poetic than hard nosed."

"And, what is that?"

"I never mentioned this to you. Before I entered the seminary I had a great love and, if I were to be in love with anyone, it would be Virginia. No one else, no one. "

"Who is Virginia?"

"Virginia is the love of my life; she died so many years ago."

Alex shuddered, but only briefly. He said she was dead. He drew philosophical lessons from every event or subject; a modern day Socrates. "Love itself is such a powerful force. It's not easily assigned to the same historical dust bin that swallows everything else."

"Meaning?"

"Well, love obliterates the ending of time in relationships. People die, people move away, but their presence never dissipates. They remain engaged, part of our tissue and we part of their tissue."

Alex was excited by his explanation. "Give me an example."

"I often wonder, for example, what Virginia is thinking? When I kissed Celia on the cheek, what, if anything, was Virginia thinking? Resenting? Happy for me? Angry at being shunted aside because she feels that my love belongs exclusively to her? We have eternal souls; we don't die, even though we used that word. We always remain alive and engaged, more engaged than ever. Does she feel neglected? Cast into oblivion? I just wonder. That gives me another reason to exercise greater self-discipline. I hope she understands. You see, Alex, I'm faithful to her. Of course, I am talking in a kind of poetic way, not in the concrete terms of human jealousy or anything like that. I just believe that you cannot cut the lifeline between souls who have had deep interpersonal and sexual relations. Something has to continue. I could as well have said, is she delighted for me? Does she wish I had another love in addition to the love we had? Does a mother pass on and forget about her children she leaves behind, loses interest in them? Unthinkable. Just as unthinkable that lovers could ever, ever be separated. Impossible."

Alex had never seen him so passionate. It made her feel that every priest should be a lover first, before ordination, as impractical as that sounds. She understood him completely. A man, who happens to be a priest--that is how she defined him. Clergy protestations to the contrary notwithstanding, and admitting her limited knowledge, priests are not exempt from the general rule: The love of God is manifested in our love of neighbor. Not love in some angelic form, but in the carnal. We are not angels, for God's sake. She needed to constantly remind her patients of this fundamental human umbilical chord. Isolation from the carnal leads one to devastation. She had no doubt that what he was experiencing and admitting, many other priests experience and hide.

Alex did not understand Celia's strategy, but strategic thinking was her strength. Her retreats were always tactical. He would soon be hurt. She cried for him, on his behalf. Not only did she not believe Celia was repentant, but her fear was that over time she would entice him back on the pretext: "Let's remain friends." The process would start all over again, each time coming closer to nothingness. Also, it merely delayed any chance Alex might have of bringing him happiness. That is the gift she wanted to bestow on him.

Of course, she was not all innocence either, but at least her deviousness was in a good cause, his cause. She desperately wanted to see him happy, both as a priest and as a man. He was safe with her. Celia spent most of her adult life enjoying hurting men whom she enticed, then threw away. But it is also important to understand that she enjoyed the sex. It's not as if besides hating men she also hated the sex she siphoned from them. She was far more complicated than that.

If she succeeded in trapping him, she would throw him away, as she did all the others. He would be her most important victim. He would be her father. Revenge would be sweet. That was a given. But, she would have to exert herself, be innovative. In spite of his masculine vulnerability, he was no pushover. He was, indeed, her life's biggest challenge. She proudly boasted she enticed by simply sitting quietly, with no expression on her face. Alex was tempted to tell her that any woman, at least any young woman, could do the same. But, if she had said that she would have been dishonest. Let's face it, Celia was special to men, for reasons that her male victims, I'm sure, never fully understood.

Alex feared that, in spite of his protestations to the contrary, he would now be drawn ever deeper into Celia's web, at a time when he appeared to be moving away from her. Alex feared she would win in this high stakes game of sexual roulette, regardless of what she did or knew, regardless of his heightened defenses. Celia remained the mistress of all she surveyed.

Alex had to devise a plan. She was strong on determination but weak on strategy. She hated Celia more than ever. Her hate was metastasizing. She saw destruction on the horizon. He deserved happiness and the love of a woman truly devoted to him. He would not find it with Celia. She simply was not that kind of woman, not now, not ever. Alex could give him what he needed. She knew that. She prayed that he would come to the same conclusion.

CHAPTER TWELVE

Her next entry, dated November 1, showed her schizophrenia.

"Gregory has kept away from me since I made that damn phone call. Even in church he averts his eyes so that I can't see the lust in them. I'm just thinking in prose. He says the vow of celibacy has never worked, does not work and will not work, and yet, as a priest, he intends to keep the vow. Now, tell me what kind of nonsense is that? He thinks he's being cute by telling me that. In this very diary, I have already written many times that he is screwing with my head. Let me repeat that accusation. After all, there is bedrock evidence I have for accusing him to the authorities. Here is a man, a priest, whose task is to straighten out people's heads, screwing their heads. What do you think of that? What would any reasonable person, decent person, especially a Catholic, think of that?

I do have to admit that he has had plenty of opportunity to get me in bed. I could not have been more inviting. That's weird. He's weird. He also says that since I do not have a love bond with Jack, I could file for an annulment. Now, you tell me, is he simply giving me information that as a Catholic I need in my non-marriage circumstances? Or, more likely, is he waiting for me to be free before he shows his true intentions? The latter is likely because then, he reasons, I would never be able to say that he ruined my marriage so he could get at me. Wouldn't that be neat for him! Then, he could have me without any bad conscience. Isn't that the definition of hypocrisy? I am up to his logic and his tricks. Anyway, how do I make contact with him now and save face? I really messed up. I'll talk to Alex. Maybe she can come up with an idea."

She asked Alex to chat with him and invite him to her place, where she would 'accidentally' drop by to return a cake plate she had borrowed for her husband's birthday party. "He will never suspect a thing. This way, with you present, he's not going to launch into a tirade against me for the way I behaved, and I will be as charming as I can be, to clear up the atmosphere."

Alex was very reluctant to play a role in getting them back together. She wanted him for herself. After all, he had already begun to notice her. She bought two more short skirts. It's not that he ogled or anything, but his eyes did fall on her legs several times during that luncheon. Once again, he was simply being a male. She did not gather anything more from his attention, but she did hope for more. Celia was her competitor, a powerful competitor indeed. To be quite frank about this, she wanted to get him in bed before Celia did, because she knew that in that department she would be dynamite. Whenever Celia dropped her cute little girl façade Alex could see the sexual power ooze out of her. It had nothing to do with her body, which (and she had seen her naked many times) was nothing men would give more than a passing glance, in that area she beat her hands down. No, it was something else; some kind of kinetic energy Celia displayed when she started talking about intimacy. It was becoming increasingly difficult to be her best friend. An invisible barrier stood between them now. Celia had not sensed this at the time. In fact, almost to the very end she was unaware that Alex had ceased to be her friend. Her discovery of the truth must have been terrible for her. Alex did not try to minimize the pain of betrayal, and would always have to admire her for her trust. Alex's deceptions, however morally based, haunt her.

Celia rarely, by the way, ever talked about love. Love was something she did not believe in. "I don't say love does not exist, but it is rare. Why not just say 'I want to bed you girl,' and do away with all this hypocrisy." That was her unshakable philosophy, and she was consistent in living it out. "Free love should be adopted by all the churches. Don't the priests say, Faith, hope and Love, and the greatest of these is Love?" That was as close as she ever got to talking about love.

Whenever Celia discussed sex, sensual feelings coursed through Alex's body. She created that kind of atmosphere around her. She recalled several times, after talking with Celia, she ran home, got in bed and imagined intimacy. She would start all these fires and leave them to others to put out. That was her essence and she gloried in it. She was powerful but, like a meteor, a brilliant flash in the sky; not an enduring star that one can track night after night. Once again, let me stress that she miraculously did all these things and continued to maintain her nice little girl image at the church. That was a miracle in itself, but not the spiritual kind. She was a temptress on a crusade to find her father and humiliate him. Her dangerous hissing was unmistakable and unsettling. Shelly pictured it beautifully:

> Wake the serpent not - lest he
> Should not know the way to go -
> Let him crawl which yet lies sleeping
> Through the deep grass of the meadow!
> Not a bee shall hear him creeping
> Not a May-fly shall awaken
> From its cradling blue-bell shaken
> Not the starlight as he's sliding
> Through the grass with silent gliding.

Alex wondered what there was in her that was always willing to do Celia's bidding. Why was she always the supplicant? Here she was, actually agreeing to invite him to her house so that Celia could find a way to win him back. How could that happen? They say that evil attracts. Was she actually evil? And if she was, what the hell was Alex doing cooperating with her against her own interest? She thought of seeing a shrink, but we ran out of time. She was on a stage, not being Alex, but being Celia. Is that what was happening to her? Did she really want to be her, to see in multi-chroicat splashes of color her face in her face? Is that why she actually agreed to go along with Celia's plan to invite him for dinner? Psychologist, heal thyself. Well, at least the identification with her did have a legitimate side, was a legitimate fantasy, really. What woman would not want to be the most sought after female in the universe?

CHAPTER THIRTEEN

Alex invited Gregory for early dinner, earlier than Celia suggested; that would give them more time to get to know each other. "Say, five pm?" She thought he might hesitate but he did not. In fact, he said, "I feel very comfortable with you. That luncheon gave us an opportunity to know each other better. As you can imagine, I was a bit wary of women after the way Celia acted. Perhaps I should say, reacted. My kiss on her cheek was not much more than I do after every Mass to many women. I did hug her, perhaps, a bit tighter than I should have done. I like Celia. It's just that she is exaggerating both the tone and the content of our visit."

His statement was very consoling for Alex. They were now buddies. Being buddies, she thought, was a very good foundation for a more permanent relationship. Celia would pass, she would still be there. To that end Alex dedicated herself. What he never experienced with Celia he would never miss. She had been told, and she believed, that her body was beautiful. That should help her reach her goal before he gets a taste of Celia.

Alex realized she needed to rely on the subtle. For this visit she highlighted her breasts. She had to do it in such a way as not to be too obvious. She thought that a light, lacy blouse tucked in at the waist would do it.

Alex was not trying to seduce him in the sense that she wanted to bed down at any cost, or that she was trying to get him to break his vows. She just wanted to be an option for him if he should one day decide to replace his vision of Virginia with a real woman. If so, she simply wanted to be that woman. She was convinced that she would have made him happy.

As he walked in, he smiled and said, "I left the rectory a bit early because I didn't know just how long it would take to get here." With that he gave her a hug. He was happier than she had seen him for some weeks. Perhaps, at that point in time, he was relieved that he had finally begun to detach himself from Celia. It's funny how little things one would not even notice with other folks, one is very sensitive to in a person you love. Alex enjoyed the swishing sound of his trousers brushing against her furniture.

Alex remembered that when she first saw him in the Church

she was not at all impressed. That particular day she was late for Mass; so late she missed the sermon. It wasn't until the Procession after Mass that she took note of him. There was something about the way he walked that appealed to her. He was someone who knew what he wanted and where he was going. It was not an arrogant walk, just quietly confident. As he made his way up along the aisle he smiled here and there at the parishioners. Since she had arrived late for Mass, she was standing at the end of the pew. He smiled directly at her, making a little wave with his hand, a greeting designed just for her. Everyone had the same impression, so he was instantly popular.

Oh to be the proverbial fly on the wall of each parishioner's imagination, the men and the women, even the children. Absolutely everyone gravitated toward him. He became, in just a few short weeks, a kind of superstar in our small town of Andover, an enclave of affluent intelligentsia located on the outskirts of metropolitan Boston. He was not seeking popularity. In fact, his light step, with head in clouds, elegantly unassuming, gave just the opposite impression. He appeared genuinely unaware of the kind of reaction he evoked in all of them. Celia knew she had to have him, the biggest prize in Andover, the center of the universe. Where better to capture such a prize than in this paradise of discretion, where sophisticated elegance supported unique lifestyles?

Alex's heart lifted at the sight of him in her living room. As she took his coat, their hands brushed. She wanted to hold him. "Would you like some wine or something warm to drink while my dinner readies?"

He drove his hand along the contours of his neck. "Some tea, please."

They moved to the kitchen area. In a few moments she was bending over him, pouring hot water from the kettle onto a tea bag. She inhaled his showered skin, the scent of his light cologne. It was intoxicating. Otherwise why was she giddy? Doesn't wine induce giddiness?

He glanced up to thank her; their eyes interlocked, an enchanted moment of closeness. The soft kitchen light picked up blond strands of her hair. He noticed and stared a bit. Then, self-consciously, he turned away. As his lips brushed along the cup's rim she experienced a sensual titillation, imagining them moistly brushing the nape of her neck. Resting his chin in the palm of his hands, he asked if she had music we could listen to "sort of in the background." As he usually dined alone, his company was soft music. She pointed to the stack of CDs. "Choose something you like." He chose Vivaldi's *The Four Seasons*.

As she busied herself preparing the food, his eyes fell on her, gently, an innocent attention, a little boy waiting for his mother to feed him. He was obviously very comfortable in her presence. At one point, he put an arm around her shoulders and said, "You are such a kind person." He switched themes, prompted perhaps by the music. "You know, I envy folks who find a lasting love at an early age, and receive God's gift of a very long life together. What is more beautiful to observe? What a joy, what a work of art that must be!" He stood beside the bay window staring at the unseen, the object of his meditation, absorbed, no doubt, in searing memories.

"I agree."

"Music and love. Hypnosis." His words, in their simplistic beauty, poured from the fountains of his mind in a steady, modest stream. Of course, he had found such a love, no doubt the object of his present thoughtful meditation. Her death, in one violent sweep, deprived him of life and love and liberty. Alex knew that he would never be free without her. She simply wanted to make his life more bearable. That would have been her gift to him; the reward for his gift to her.

He was hardworking, a popular priest, but he was vulnerable to the romantic image of a close relationship, a reality, amorphous at best. He needed to recover from young love, a young love that might have taken on a totally or partially different configuration over the years. Alex would never say that to him. Even if she did, he would reject such a scenario out of hand. Virginia was nineteen when she died. How lucky for her that in the mirror of his own mind he saw her eighteen-year-old face and form forever. He needed to fill the void she left, but that never happened because he ran out of time. Alex was not going to judge that that was good or bad. He could tell her now that he is with Virginia. Perhaps, he will give her such a sign from the forever. She always expected him to wrap himself in fog and settle over her bed, speaking to her.

He loved Virginia always. This, at times, in some minds could cause a certain tension and diminution of dedication to the priesthood. But he totally dismissed the validity of such a dichotomy. Like all of us, he knew ambivalence. The amazing thing is that, in spite of this, perhaps because of this, he was a far better priest and pastor than any they had ever experienced. This would be, actually, a strict interpretation of his essence. A more liberal one was uttered at a private soiree at the Country Club, where his birthday was celebrated. He was a prominent Andover attorney, who, in addition to being a competent trial lawyer, had been a classmate of Humphrey Bogart at Phillips Academy, Andover's pride and joy. He toasted Father Gregory. "As Bogey used to say, the best damn thing about you is that which we do not, as yet, know about you."

Many have questioned the attribution to Bogart, but no one disagreed that it applied to Father Gregory. They were continually surprised and pleased at the depth of his casual but penetrating remarks.

Alex joined him at the table and they lunched. The sun filtering through the curtain panels caught her hair again. This time he commented. "You must thank the sun for making your hair look so nice." He admired beauty wherever and whenever he found it and she was pleased that part of her was part of what he admired. He smiled at her and her world dazzled. Their eyes interlocked; their lives were being drawn together in an ever-growing bond, twisting and turning in a helix of, at least, companionship; at most, the beginning of untarnished love.

Referencing their previous conversation in which he said he was looking for the right woman, her head tilted toward his shoulder as she asked him, "I would think that you have no difficulty finding such a person. If you did, would you leave the priesthood and marry?"

She saw a mild amusement in his eyes.

"Well, you need not answer if you'd rather not. It's really a rather personal question. I'm sorry."

He raised both hands to his shoulders, "Oh, no! That's a fair question. The answer is that I met Virginia when I was a young man. She died before she reached the age of nineteen. I guess you could say that I have been unconsciously searching for her ever since. Perhaps, in one part of my brain, I do not believe she is dead. I look for her everywhere I go. Perhaps I want to experience that again. But there is great safety in the realization that I will not."

Alex took some comfort in his remarks because, knowing that he would never violate his vows, she would never need to worry about competition. In one sense, she was all he had, the only person with whom he was close. If she could not be his wife, she could be his confidant and she would love and savor every minute of it.

She threw out a question to further understand his mindset. "Does the love of Virginia ever interfere with your work?"

He glanced out the kitchen window for a bit. Her unfulfilled yearnings and memories of what was do take up a bit of her time. It has not been easy. But is that interference? No more, probably, than it would the wife of a dead husband. How could a woman ever forget her husband if they had a beautiful marriage? Should she? Not really. She didn't think anyone, not even the Church should demand the elimination of our past, for our past is an essential part of whom we are. So, if the Church is happy with a priest then it is happy with the composite that he is, not picking on little parts to dissect."

The door bell rang, and Celia arrived with flair, entering the driveway at far too great a speed, slamming her brakes to a jolting stop right at the front door. Alex experienced no feelings of welcoming. Her entrance resembled more that of a thief in the dark of night, than an invited guest. She feigned great surprise at seeing Gregory, walked straight to him and kissed him on the cheek. "Father Gregory, what a nice surprise. How have you been?"

Alex could see that he was uncomfortable, but he remained pleasant. "Well, thank you. And you?"

"Fine." Then, she turned to me. "Forgive my intrusion. I just popped in to pick up that pie plate. It's my favorite and Jack has been begging for another pie."

Her mind wrapped in a haze. Celia's every intrusion now unsettled her, but she kept her cool. Neither noticed her interrupted breathing.

Celia's rhythms of deviousness droned on, sending him a message. "Oh, yes, I am fine, but I've been very troubled by some stupid things I've done." She paused and turned her head away from him. "Have you ever had that experience?"

"Oh yes", he said, "many times."

Then, she played her card and won. "Father Gregory, tomorrow is my birthday and Jack is out of town. I want to take you to out for lunch and pick your brains. I can meet you at the rectory about 10 and off we go to a wonderful place in the White Mountains! What do you say? I promise to have you back by 4 pm."

He simply said, "Yes" It was clearly a "Yes" that wanted to calm troubled waters, that would heal an unintended wound.

A triumphant look flooded her face. "Great."

Alex died another one of those little deaths. Celia's innate sensuality sprayed itself over every object, animate and inanimate, in the room. As she took the pie plate from Alex's hands she continued playacting. "Well, let me leave you two to enjoy your evening." Turning to Gregory, she said, "I look forward to tomorrow." With that, leaving behind a tornado ripping through the avenues of my psyche, she abruptly left us.

Alex looked to him to see signs of disgust in his face, or hear some words of cynicism; there was nothing. He simply said, "Well, life sure takes some strange twists and turns."

One bit of consolation surfaced when she asked if he was really going to have lunch with her. "I am riding off into the sunset; but I want to do it one horizon at a time. Safer that way." He moved to a sofa closer to me. "But, since we're on the subject, let me say that Celia is a problem for me. She has to have what she wants, and that is dangerous because men do not know how to fight against female demands. They exhaust themselves trying to be gentlemen and respectful even in the face of their onslaughts. Not her fault; not even a fault. Just nature, that's all. We're all born with a different DNA. She is what she is. I blame her for nothing. I have to deal with it."

He was trying to get Celia out of his life without causing her to erupt. Alex needed to leave it at that. Celia was her competition, but a less powerful competitor than she previously imagined.

He did not mention her again in what turned out to be a long evening of getting to know each other. They spoke about where they were from, where they went to school, what their families were like. It was really nice, yet Alex feared, deep down, that Celia had won him back. There she was, in an old skirt and a loose blouse, with no makeup, walking in, grabbing the prize and walking right out again. Alex tried not to hate her, but it was difficult.

Gregory later said, "We should feel sorry for her," but that was not easy. She did not share his confidence that he was on his way out of her life. She feared he would not be able to resist her charms. The peculiar intense sensuality that commanded the attention of so many men fostered their lust and desires was a major power in her arsenal.

The one thing Alex had won, however, was his enduring friendship. From that day on she called him almost every evening for a chat. She asked him, "Am I imposing on you?"

"I love it," he said. "I'm beginning to feel badly about leaving here. I've gotten to like Andover very much. I appreciate whatever you do to make life more pleasant for me. I feel selfish, like I'm imposing on you. You are a real friend."

It was clear that his only burden in being in beautiful Andover was the inimitable, hated, loved, admired, despised Celia. Alex did not have all that she wanted, but she could now spend much more time with him, and who knows where that could lead?

CHAPTER FOURTEEN

Her next entry was November 6, the day after the visit to my home.

"I had a feeling it was my lucky day. I woke up this morning, sunlight streaming through the window shutters making lovely designs on my bed, cheering me up. Today was Gregory-to-Lunch day. I was so grateful. I had high hopes that we might now be able to work things out. I felt a quickening in my pulse. I picked him up at the rectory.

"Hi, there." He has a straightforward gaze that penetrates, enhancing his bright brown eyes, his air of calm authority. He wore a denim shirt and wrinkled khakis. "Where do we eat?"

"The Alpine. You know it?"

"Oh yes, beautiful place, been there twice, but a long time ago. Good taste, lady."

The Alpine, a small but luscious restaurant, is located along the coast about an hour and a half out of town. A narrow ribbon of road brought us there. The restaurant proper is surrounded by glazed, rust-colored earthenware tubs containing a variety of colorful plants. It sits amidst large, tall promontories of blunted, gray rock. Asymmetrical in design, with a steeply canted shingled roof, it graces the landscape. I love it. My first tryst took place there. His name was Archibald, not a name that evokes romance, but he defied the odds. We were both virgins, an Innocence now gone forever. Archibald and I walked along the shoreline first, working up an appetite for food. It was so much fun. One spot had a little gazebo with railings you could lean on for gazing at the ocean below, as it slammed powerful waves that tumbled into frothy ripples on the sand. Dark patches of kelp, carried in by powerful currents, awaited the next slam to carry them back out. It reminded me of a woman giving herself to the man, awaiting his next powerful shock, his next innovation, and exposing herself to his invitation to return time and again.

There was no walk today. I did not want to push my luck. The restaurant was not crowded. They served us lobster with fresh garlic mayonnaise. Delicious. For the first half hour we skimmed the surface of our realities, focusing on the banal, like the weather, my cousin Sally, the Red Sox. "They always bring us to the edge of victory, then, bang, a disappointment."

"Yes," as if it made any difference to either of us. Circumlocution precedes circumvention. That's OK. We all do it. It's a way to either get started or to initiate the beginning of the end. The sound of his words matched the silence of his face. Inscrutable. The colors of the summer garden surrounding us kept hope alive. The passing waiters, diners, maitre' de, even in their obvious busyness, move in slow motion, almost agonizingly slow. All of us are waiting for him to say something, something substantive. Enough of the Red Sox.

He does, entering our own domain with the statement, "I'm glad to see you looking so well. You've been through a hell of a lot recently." Even in this intimate setting he had a way of remaining attractively aloof, if that's not a contradiction in terms.

"Yes," I said, "I have been through hell itself, actually."
He leaned toward me and whispered, "To the extent that I am responsible for any of your sadness and grief I am very sorry. Please believe me." Was that the beginning of reconciliation, or its ending? What do we know about anything, really?

"I want to see you happy again, well again."

He had never seen me happy. I have never been happy, unless it was before my father raped me, abused me, and incarcerated me in our beautiful-home-turned-prison. But, I have no memories prior to the rape, so I don't know, actually, if I ever had even one single, solitary day of happiness. Isn't that terrible? I think so. That's why I hate my father so much, why I live to despise him. I thought, well, on my wedding day I will be happy. After all, who ever heard of an unhappy bride on the day of her wedding? Even if she regrets marrying the guy, a wedding is a wedding is a wedding. We women love preparing for it, dressing for it, walking down the isle, even if it leads to hell.

His voice echoed in my reverie. "I came here to tell you the truth; otherwise I would not have come. I trust you believe me."

"Oh, yes, "even though I intended and he knew I intended that reply to be provisional, just as we are all provisionally who we are.

I believed him, up to a point. He has certainly changed my life. I go from admiring his intellect to seriously questioning his honesty. I experience him through bouts of shimmering erotic fantasies. Being in love is a whole new experience for me. I keep waiting for him to suggest that we meet in the park, but he doesn't. Finally, frustrated, I said "Well, why don't we begin to meet in the park again, just establish a solid relationship sans emotions? What do you think?"

He paused for a long time, looking down at his plate, tightly pursing his lips, tugging at his shirt sleeves. I squelched the urge to reach out and touch him.

He raised his head and looked at me with those cool and distant eyes, his expression wary. "Celia, to be very honest, I'm afraid to do anything that would lead to a misunderstanding with you. That would destroy both of us. Maybe not today, maybe not tomorrow, but eventually you will erupt again. I just can't face it anymore. I'm sorry. I have already caused you a great deal of harm. I want to stop now, to avoid any unpleasantness in either of our lives. I need to focus on my work."

I couldn't argue with his reasoning and I knew it was too early to tell if there was a chance. As I sat there within touching distance I wanted him more than ever. I admired him more than ever. I had to win him back. That's all I knew at that moment. I would love to avoid this pain of not having him all to myself by dipping into hallucinatory cannabis, but I need to keep my wits about me. In Dante's Inferno, heaven and hell are right next door to each other. Dante meandered through hell in order that he might have greater knowledge. My hell has not given me that. Only confusion. He and I are running out of time. I know that, of course. I suspect he knows that also. Dante put it well, "The time we are allotted soon expires."

Anyway, there are some promising signs. We were together again today. Even in his decision to avoid meetings that might end in what he called misunderstanding, but really meant intimacy. I am no fool. His very concern was itself a message that he cared for me. So, today I did get some consolation. I did not want to disturb the moment, did not want to jeopardize the future, so I remained calm and cooperative. It was only a tactic. I really wanted to scream out, but I held back. My tactic now is to break through his self-imposed illusion and façade. The fact is, he really wants me. I need to be patient. I want to snare him because he wants to be snared. He cannot hide that from me. I don't think he is purposely hiding that fact from me; not at all. He is confused, afraid, unsure--not so much of himself, as of his true desires and feelings. He needs more time to sort it out, think about it, and ponder. He does not know this but his time is running out. This will be my final attempt. After this, le deluge. Or, should I say *après moi le deluge*?

I looked at him closely as we finished our meal, to divine in his facial expressions and body language his true and unvarnished feelings and desires. Previously, the arching of his eyebrows telegraphed his mood before he uttered a word; now, he was silent and noncommittal. He gazed absently out of the restaurant's large window at the ocean, with an occasional "Oh. Wow. Beautiful," pretending he saw an ocean denizen unusual. He uses silence very skillfully.

I leaned forward and placed my cheek on his shoulders, entreating. I said, 'OK, let's just stay in touch and see how things go. I'm terribly sorry for the awful things I said about you. I do truly apologize. You are a good man. I needed to get used to the idea and I believe that's happening. I hope it's not too late for me, for us. I'm unable to look into the future. Right now I have no idea how this day will end. I feel I've lived my life already. Perhaps it's time to bring it to an end. That's how I feel."

I reached over, gripping his fingers for support, but they did not respond with any strength. He glanced lovingly, but did not respond further. He took my hand as we stood; we walked out together. The ride home seemed too short. There was so much left unsaid, but the atmosphere did not prompt more than the paltry bits we covered. As we made our way back to Andover, I half dozed in the comfort of his presence. He was silent, but warm, letting the soft music do the talking. As we reached the rectory, he sighed. "I wish I could say more right now, but I dare not. Let us be. Let us be kind. Let me wish you a beautiful day."

I found myself pleading. "When will I see you again?"

He threaded his hands in his pockets, his eyes toward the sky. "Soon, I hope." His words echoed in the narrow space we occupied. He was harboring emotions he did not want to share with me in that sliver of time. "I need to go now." His words were barely audible. We parted. There was no kiss on the cheek, no hug, just a smile. He moved away from me, chin high, steps strong. His skin flushed with whatever emotions he was feeling.

I managed, "I'll be waiting for you."

He did not reply. His nose curled and his lips twitched as he flashed a last wave. Then he simply disappeared into the bowels of his residence. I was a rose shriveled by a blast of arctic air. His quiet dignity shamed me. It had not been so long ago that I had a proprietary lock on his emotions. Now, the pillars of that strength were crumbling, shattered by the blast of my stupidity. He, for his part, walked off, his emotional strength intact, tempered as finest steel.

I watched his departure with terror. I was only now coming to understand his bedrock integrity. I only wish that my understanding had come earlier. If it had, we would now be living together somewhere, lost in love. It's not too late. He can be, I'm sure, after all, very lustful, given the right atmosphere. I will create that atmosphere. I am sleepless with the muddle of it all, trying to form at least a half-sketched plan, something flawless. I know how to dance the dance of the sexes. I am very sophisticated. If I cannot snare a sexually deprived celibate priest, there is nothing left for me to live for. For Jack. No, not for Jack. You see, Jack, believe it or not, does not need me. He is pleasant, good looking, amorphous, able to fit in anywhere, or, if need be, nowhere. In short, he doesn't need me. Look at the time! It's late. I'm going to pour myself some chilled red wine and drown my thoughts in it."

CHAPTER FIFTEEN

Some time had passed after Celia described their meeting to me. Alex felt then that danger lurked right around the corner of her mind. Celia's inner thoughts were rife with signs of violence. She was afraid. Three days before Thanksgiving Alex invited Father Gregory for Thanksgiving dinner, just the two of them. He was flying off to Italy the following day, taking a break before the busy Advent season began. She was too late. "I promised my sister. It's kind of a tradition on Thanksgiving for the entire family to get together. My nieces and nephews would be terribly disappointed if I do not show up."

"I understand."

He saved the day. "What about Saturday, after the evening Mass?

"Great."

Alex was ready for his visit. She fixed her hair so that it tossed around with the slightest movement of air, imitating what she had seen in TV ads. In honor of the season she wore an orange blouse, ruffled about the neck, together with a silk skirt that clung to her legs. Her mood now was not so much to bed with him, as to protect him. It finally got through to her that he had no intention of living with a woman, not even her wonderful, beautiful self! As Celia needed to get real so did she.

She heard the gravel crunching arrival of his car as he pulled into the driveway. She wanted to be calm, so she ran her hands over her hair and along her face, as if that would do the trick, and met him at the door. He stood back, his arms spread eagle. "Hi, you look nice enough to hug," which he then proceeded to do. He was very cheerful, giving Alex a kiss on the cheek. Celia's complaint about 'only a kiss on the cheek,' did not resonate with Alex. She was grateful for any sign of affection. The feel of his lips anywhere on her body was comforting, appreciated.

Alex had prepared a full Thanksgiving meal and he really enjoyed it. He was now so comfortable with her that he carried a couple of shirts and a pair of jeans to hang in her closet. His lack of romantic feelings was offset by his use of her home as his home away from home. She simply thanked God for her good fortune and settled for lower expectations. Alex did not want, as

Celia was in the process of doing, to lose what she had. He made his fondness for her very obvious; lots of hugs and innocent kisses. Her home was a haven for his troubled soul. She was beginning to experience a wife's joy. Naturally, she would have appreciated the marital compensations that accompany such devotion! Oh well, Gandhi slept in the same bed with his wives, but did not engage in sex. So no new ground is being broken. After the meal they retired to the living room and had a second wonderful evening. Alex would miss him while he was in Italy.

As expected, Celia called to find out if Gregory had shown up for dinner.

"Yes."

"Well, the bastard didn't even call me. I think he's just playing cute. I don't know if he's pretending he's some sort of super jock, super morality guy or what. I ought to just dump him altogether. He's too damn complicated."

Alex's focus now was on the rage that was building up in her body. She lived with stalking fears, listened intently to every word, seeking hints of her plan. Her voice wreaked over her incoherent decisions and planning.

"Well, Celia, as I've suggested before, if you feel that way, why don't you just do it."

"Oh, I don't know. Maybe I want to beat him at his game."

"Wouldn't it be better to use your time either working things out with Jack, or leaving him? He does have some rights you know."

She did pause when Alex said that. "Yeah, you're right. I'm just wasting my life. I'll probably end up losing Jack. I'm getting old you know! At my age they just want something on the side. They marry the younger ones."

Alex laughed. "Old? What in the name of heaven are you talking about? You look like a school girl." This was the first time she ever heard Celia talk this way about herself. She was beginning to collapse deep down inside. Eventually, it would worm its way to the surface. That would be the day of darkness.

"Thanks, Alex. I guess I'm just upset over this whole thing. I think I'll take your advice and call him when he gets back from Italy and tell him it's over."

The reality, of course, is that, from his perspective, it was truly over already, but she was unable to pick up all the obvious signals Gregory tossed out at her by the armful.

"This affair has put a big strain on me. Sometimes I look in the mirror and don't recognize myself, the person I used to be."

"That happens to all of us, Celia. Just part of coping with life, I think."

She laughed. "I only enjoy men playing doctor."

She had it almost right when she said she no longer recognized herself in the mirror. That was her fundamental problem. Her life was a variation on that theme. Her traumatic childhood disabled her normal psychological development. She never became a person with whom, as an adult, she could identify. The abuse she suffered from her father erased any internal memory of her childhood prior to the first rape. Her growing realization of the implications of this tragedy positioned her dead center of the most threatening period of her life. Her attraction to Gregory spurred her consciousness, fired her desire for real love. She would either seek her true self and be saved, or she would self-destruct.

Early the next morning she called. "I'll wait till hell freezes over before I'll call him. If he gets in touch with you, let me know."

CHAPTER SIXTEEN

Celia's next entry was on Nov. 29th.

"When I got home last night Jack was there being charming, his fist full of the most glorious red roses I have ever seen. I know it was some sort of attempt to revive our relationship. Even though I know that the relationship is dead, I do appreciate the fact that at least he made an attempt. That's more than I can say for this sexually dysfunctional priest. Added to this is the guilt trip I have for fooling around with him in the first place. If he could at least make the guilt trip worthwhile, I could live with it! I'm going to call him and tell him to drop this bloody charade. If he's not man enough to show me that I mean something to him he's got to go!"

Her next entry was that of December 2ndth:

"Gregory came back from Italy today after a ten-day trip. He probably found some nice Italian girl who thinks he's the greatest stud ever. I don't know how he gets away with it, how the Church allows it. He has no morals whatsoever. How the hell did he ever get ordained? I sure don't know. The parish secretary told me he's all tanned. That will be an improvement. When he left, his face was pale and his eyes puffy. He said that our situation leaves him tired and edgy. Well, let me tell you, it leaves me in a far worse state."

Celia called Alex the next day from her office. "Gregory got in last night. I had no intention of calling him first, but I did. And, how does he start out his conversation? Does he say, 'Hi, It's nice to hear your voice again, or 'I missed you, Can we meet in the park today?' Does he tell me about Italy, whom he met, or anything? At least I'd have some talking points at work. No, he did not. He said, 'I've had a much needed rest. I love Italy. It brings me back to my roots, so to speak. I guess all nationalities feel that way when they visit the homeland of their parents or grandparents.' Now, Alex, tell me, what the hell does that have to do with anything. I didn't need a lecture on tourism."

Alex did not respond. She let her finish. For the first time in the entire history of our relationship, she had something to say to her without embellishment.

"Then, the bastard said, "Well, Celia, I'll see you at our next parish council meeting and, of course, at church. Let me see, the next council meeting is on January 10th."

I felt so demeaned by that remark. I've got to wait before I can see him again? He has become emperor? Well let me tell you something, Alex, he will become an emperor without clothes. Just who the hell does he think he is? There are guys lined up to get at me, and this bastard tells me I have to wait a couple of weeks just to get some hand-in-the-pocket, leaning-against-a-chair conversation with him at the parish council? That is sheer, unadulterated B.S.. Then he comes on with, 'I'll stay in touch,' and practically tried to hangs up on me."

"What did you say?"

"I told him I don't need him, that he's just an unfaithful priest, period, and I want nothing more to do with him. "

"What did he say?"

"He didn't get a chance to say anything. I hung up on him."

"Well, Celia, if you hung up on him, you don't really know how that conversation might have ended."

"What advice would you give?"

Alex flexed the muscles of her new dimension. "Celia, you need to start adjusting to the new realities. He no longer wants to continue the sort of relationship he had with you. Why not accept this and adjust to it? Accept it and move on."

"Move on to what? Jack? Give me a break. He lives in his own world."

She had never been so bold with Celia, but our relationship was now becoming linear, after a year of constantly going in circles?

"Let it rest, Celia, let it rest." She waited for a mini explosion. It came. She was no longer afraid.

"Damn it, Alex, are you taking his side?"

"I'm not taking anyone's side. I'm simply interested in your welfare. I honestly feel that if you do not drop this relationship, a relationship he does not want, you will do a lot of harm to yourself. You have to face this problem and beat it. If you do not defeat the problem, it will defeat you. Believe me."

"There you go with that analysis crap again. I don't need that. I need help.

"In this case, Celia, they are one and the same thing."

Alex did not panic. From this day onward, the three had to get on a reality track. Celia had set him up and now she wanted to tear him down because he was not having sex with her. What a turned-on-its-head kind of world she lived in. Alex used to hate her; now, she's beginning to pity her. She also adjusted to the fact that they were not yet out of the woods. Celia was still capable of inflicting a great deal of damage. Actually, she had barely begun. But Alex was ready. She was now prepared to cope with any eventuality. She had, in the course of this tragic soap opera, changed, strengthened. As for Father Gregory, he was always strong, never afraid; just sad. The impact of Celia's threats was coming to an end.

Soon she would act. When? Alex did not know, but the inevitability of it all was certain. If the coming problem took the form of accusations, he was resigned. He never defends himself. His reasons for seeking female companionship, his lingering connection with a dead girl, were so complicated that he would not try to explain them to anyone. He would just say, "She's telling the truth."

Alex prayed for him, getting down on her knees, raising her arms to the heavens and pleading with God to spare him any suffering. She had already adjusted to the fact that neither she nor Gregory could do any more than keep themselves sane, pray for the best. Their unity was solid, unbreakable. Each was prepared to surrender life to save the other. It was more than miraculous. Another word had to be coined for this trans-formation. Trans-mutation? Perhaps, because when Alex looks in the mirror now, her eyes look straight back at her, either not finding the old Alex or delighted that the real one came back home.

There remained, of course, the triangular relationship, the sense that somehow or other they would never become disentangled. But, there was also the sense that they were on the right track, che sera, sera, even tragedy. Alex remained realistic, her feet firmly planted on solid ground. She never believed that we were more than a heartbeat away from her le deluge. The difference, this time, is that her world and his world were now straight and clear. Death no longer presented a serious challenge. In an odd way, isn't this exactly what the Church has been telling us for centuries? Peace comes with a clear conscience. How simple, how true, how profoundly true, even in its depth and simplicity. Amazing. Look at what happened. Gregory got through his fleeting brush with danger; I got through my need to bed him.

Celia remained the problem. God allows us our moments, even long ones, of foolishness. He allows us, in religious terms, to pick ourselves up after a fall. She still had a chance to do this. However, it was difficult for Alex, having read so many novels, seen so many movies, and studied so much psychology, that she ever would. In her professional judgment, tragedy was inevitable, that it would strike us and strike us hard. And yet there was equanimity. Alex must emphasize to all her patients that a good conscience, a determination to maintain integrity at any cost, saves us all. Now, when she sees, writ large on ghetto buildings, the inscriptions JESUS SAVES, she no longer ridicules. She no longer pities the poor and unwashed masses that have nothing else hopeful to say. She has become a member of their non-establishment Church.

CHAPTER SEVENTEEN

The next entry is Nov. 30th.

"I decided to call him. Just to flush him out. I reminded him that he never said he would not call me. He apologized for not calling, saying that he felt we needed space to reverse where we had been going. I think a man should not be worried about things like that. He should be more aggressive. Anyway, I'm stuck with the way he is, because I want him. He has been nothing but a series of disappointments. This relationship is going to be short-lived."

She pretended he had called her, giving a version of events that differed from her notes. "The bastard called me. Listen to this incredible nonsense. He had the gall to say, 'Celia, I really don't think we should see each other anymore. It's too emotional. We would just begin another round of ups and downs.' She paused, but her breathing was heavy and dense."

"So, you really feel this time that it's over?"

She screamed, "Over! It never even got started. That's the whole damn thing. It's just been a big stupid exercise on my part, a fast trip to nowhere. He got freebies without giving me a damn thing in return, except frustration."

Alex listened as she let off steam. She said, "Celia, that seems a bit unfair. I mean, it takes two to tango."

She screamed again in a louder voice. "Are you taking this bastard's side? I guess he'll be in your panties pretty soon."

Alex remained quiet. There was an awkward pause. Then Celia said, "Sorry. I'm all upset. You are right. I played right along with his little game, so I'm partially responsible. But, that's never going to happen again."

Alex was not convinced. If Celia had spoken in her normal calm, collected voice, she might have been convinced. But she had learned never to believe her when she spoke in anger, especially about a man. Alex remained alert. She had far from had her final say on this matter. Constant vigilance was the key.

Celia scoffed. "I don't think that fool knows what an apology is. He can preach all about it from the pulpit, but he learned it from books. These priests never have to apologize to anybody. They think they are God Almighty. I know his type. He better not mess with my head. I can beat him at his own game. I'm much more experienced. He's a novice to life. He has a lot to learn. Glad I have you there, Alex. Thanks."

Although Alex's duplicity with her was coming to an end, she continued to determine the course of events, moving the three of them further into darkness. She was not alone in accepting responsibility. There remained things for Alex to do, likewise. She needed to give him space to evolve our relationship in a way that did not threaten him, did not make him feel he was betraying the church. She settled for that because she faced the reality that he would remain a priest, whatever his personal opinion of celibacy and priesthood. There had been only one love in his life. There would continue to be only one love in his life. Alex had to internally accept that reality. She would settle for close friendship. If anything more developed it would be an unexpected bonus.

It was clear from her demeanor and welcoming that he had "access" to her. This must have crossed his mind many times. She had no doubt, viewing him as a virile male bursting with love and affection, that there had to be moments when he wanted to bed her down. That would be normal. To be offended at such thoughts on his behalf would be the equivalent of being offended that he existed as a male.

When Alex looks back on it now, of course, she sees that not only Celia had refused to face reality. They were both, really, whistling in the dark. But Alex was doing something good, not evil. She needed to say this because it's true.

It was at this point that the inevitable tragedy began to unfold in some sort of order. The waiting period, one might say, was now over. As in war, the period of negotiations had drawn to a close. The battle lines were being drawn. The gods of war were in the process of assembling their mighty forces. Le deluge could faintly be seen on the far horizon. Soon, it would begin to approach and we would observe its outlines distinctly.

Alex received a phone a call from Jack, telling her that Celia had collapsed at work and appeared to be incoherent. "Her fellow-workers just dropped her off. They said the doctor could find nothing wrong with her that a couple of days rest would not cure. He diagnosed it as mental fatigue." Jack pleaded, "Could you please come out and spend some time with her? I don't know what to do. I don't think she even wants me around, to be honest."

Alex said she would and advised him to remain calm. "You and I will be able to cope with whatever it is that's bothering her. You have done all you could do to make her home bearable. Don't blame yourself for anything."

He surprised her. "Oh, I don't. I have tried, in truth. But, I need you, Alex."

"Of course."

He sighed into the telephone. "God bless you, Alex. Thank you so much I don't know what I would do without you."

She packed toiletries and a nightgown, feeling that she might need to overnight. Her fear of Celia was not dissipated, not at all, but she was able to place it on hold. When she arrived Celia was sound asleep. Jack explained that, "She's been sedated, that she may not wake up until later this evening."

"Listen, Jack, I came prepared to spend the night if you like. It's your call."

"I was hoping you might, actually. I'll sleep downstairs. You can use the guest room next to our bedroom."

Alex pulled a chair alongside Celia's bed and stood watch. About six that evening she awoke, startled, saw her and asked, "What the hell am I doing here? What the hell are you doing here? What happened?"

Alex told her that she had passed out at work. "A doctor was called. He had an ambulance take you home, gave you some sedation and put you to bed.

"When did this happen?"

"Late this morning. Jack called me and asked me to come out and stay with you. I'm going to spend the night in the guest bedroom."

She was weak, but she managed to sound an alarm. "Oh, my God, I hope I didn't go running at the mouth about anything. You know what I mean."

Alex knew exactly what she meant, but assured her that she had not. She said, not knowing it to be true or false, "No one knows anything. You didn't say anything. You just collapsed. In any case, the way you work overtime, the folks there and Jack assume you are exhausted. It's also what the doctor said, so don't worry." She was relieved.

"I was so upset about Gregory that I just fell apart. I need to get myself together. He's not worth my getting sick."

Alex lied again, but this lie had a benign purpose. She was in deep psychological trouble. They must not do or say anything to prolong her agony. "That's right."

There was a phone next to her bed. Celia pointed and said, "Call Gregory. Tell him I'm at home sick, not to call me at work until I'm back on my feet. I'll call him when I feel better."

You can see how she frustrated Alex, but she was handling it better. One second Celia is saying, "I will have nothing more to do with him," and, the next second she is saying, "Tell him I will call him when I am feeling better."

"Good idea." Alex picked up the phone and made the call. He listened quietly, and thanked me for letting him know. She explained that she was at Celia's side.

Immediately, he asked, "May I speak with her?"

Alex passed on the request. Celia hesitated and then said, "I'll talk with him." She took the phone. After a series of "Mms, she placed the phone on the receiver. "Well, maybe it's all worth it. He apologized for putting me off and promised to see me as soon as he can. He finally came to his senses." She laid her head back and remained quiet. Her ashen cheeks had turned a rosy pink as she talked with him. She fingered and fondled her hair, as if he could see here. It laid soft about her shoulders. The conversation transformed her; she looked beautiful. In a few minutes she was back to sleep, seemingly contented. She knew how to win every battle with him. Alex envied her. The Advent season was upon us. Gregory was very busy with all the ritual. Perhaps his busyness would help him handle the pressing emotional problems he faced.

Alex spent the night with Celia and left around noon the following day. She noticed a considerable change in her demeanor. Celia appeared happy and confident. Alex had no doubt that Gregory had said something over the phone that calmed her down; but she was not talking.

CHAPTER EIGHTEEN

A few words about the relationship between Celia and Jack are perfectly in order. Their story cannot be fully understood without this knowledge. Jack was a good man, a good friend, but a poor husband. She needed more than a friend in her marital bed. She needed an understanding lover, one who had the instinct to cope with her father problem. Jack tried, but did not have the instinct. She had become accustomed to his presence, his unwavering loyalty. She wanted him there, but not in her bed. His awkwardness, his frequent impotency, aroused painful images of a father figure fresh from the bed of his wife, blaming Celia, beating her when he could not perform. She was determined to prove the attractiveness of her sexuality to her husband, to her dead father, to all the male enemies she invited into her body.

Jack never complained. He blamed himself and tried to survive. He would never abandon her. Here he was, a husband who never felt comfortable tending to his wife because she wanted him 'there,' but not 'here.' There were rumors that he was unfaithful. That was such a joke. If he were seeing another woman it would be out of sheer desperation, but Celia's public image drew all the sympathy. "I don't know how she tolerates him" typified the average comment. Here was a man who had a wife who was not a wife, who was confused about who she was and where she was going, but people were now beginning to whisper, "They say he's a philanderer." Here was a woman who was abused by her father, a good and intelligent woman who suffered from pain that could not be assuaged, nor ever be adequately understood by the rest of us. There was no evil here, just fate.

She lived from day to day, wandering the earth in search of a mate who could heal her father-ravaged soul, her father-ravaged body. He lived from day to day, wondering if she had slept with some guy that morning or afternoon, wondering if she would be there tomorrow. At the same time, he knew that she was very vulnerable, that she might hurt herself, destroy herself. He stayed because if she fell from self-inflicted wounds there would be no one there for her to lean on. The truth, of course, is that he unwittingly supported her lifestyle by keeping her secret, by picking up the pieces, but not knowing, let us face it, what to do. In the former he was a success; in the latter he was a failure. Once again, let me emphasize, there was no blame here, only unsolvable problems.

From the very beginning he never was a real husband. He came into the marriage with a hefty bank account. Each agreed to retain privately the funds they had at the time of their marriage. That was a big mistake. Jack had this secret gambling life. Well, secret up to a point. She knew he liked to "spend twenty or thirty dollars" at the casino, just for fun. It took a good five years before she discovered that he had gone through over one hundred thousand dollars of his own money, and was now eating into their joint accounts. She never made a big thing of it. She never abandoned him. To me, her closest friend, perhaps her only friend, she never mentioned a word of it until she desperately need mortgage payment cash to save the house. She also kept his secrets. The male reader must understand that her pain was greater than his, even though the external view may suggest otherwise. He was ready for intimacy at the smell of his sexually potent wife. He was a male.

There is no blame there; he was acting out masculinity. She was a woman. There was no automatic turn on. She needed to be roused. He was unable to do that. Not his fault. Not her fault. Just the way it was. How sad.

And yet, she needed him. He was her rock of stability. She paid the price of that need by continuing to support his gambling habits, by faithfully returning to a marriage nest that never was a marital nest. She had, to be honest, great courage, great dedication. She would never leave him because she knew he needed her. Her occasional outbursts were born of frustration, of pain. She always experienced sorrow at the sorrow she inflicted on him. No guilt, just a situation, a mess.

Jack suffered the same kindness. He would never abandon her. His principal role, and he accepted it with full devotion, was as curator for all that was precious in her. His secondary role was to be there for her should her secret be discovered, and everyone else abandon her. He wore the mask of the happy and contented husband, and, to some extent, given all the circumstances, that was true, because he loved her and only her.

God will forgive her much. As He did on the cross, He will take the blame. She suffered her pains in silence. So did he. In that sense, they had a love for each other rare to find. He tolerated her hangovers, the short but intense periods of self-hatred she suffered after every sexual encounter that came up short of love. He understood her secret and internal struggle with the frightening images of a sexually abusive father. Jack knew this. He knew that Gregory was her only hope. He also knew Gregory would not engage. He was compassionate. He cried for her. He held her in his arms, even as she struggled to free herself from his embrace. He needed to keep her stable, to hide her indiscretions. He was the guardian of her soul. One might even say, he was her guardian angel.

He needed help because although they had a relationship of mutual dependency, she rarely engaged him in conversation. She would tell him, "Why are you always interfering in my life?"

She was right. He was right. There was no blame, just pain. Alex had many such clients. The truth is that most of them suffer from one form or other of sexual mismatching. You would be surprised how common it is. There should be a law: No one may marry unless they live with their partner for a minimum of two years, until they test their sexual compatibility. Alex's experience with Celia and Jack taught her to recognize the signs. Her intimate knowledge of their relationship resulted in helping many of her clients. She wanted Celia to be her client, but she refused to acknowledge her problem, even to herself. She scoffed at the idea. Alex did her best to convince her, but failed.

CHAPTER NINETEEN

Alex had a personal stake in all of this. She was so grateful that she had truly begun to live. No longer was she passing time, filling voids. The new freedom to live came in the nick of time. She had a mission that only a liberated person could handle. She needed to protect him. They were nearing Celia's final act of irrationality. Alex had no doubt about it. Both she and Gregory were ready for battle, whatever happened, whatever the result. They were not simply sleepwalking their way through. They were on the alert, watching her every mood. They were not against her, simply afraid of what she might do, not only to them, but to herself. Previously, Alex had misread her. Now, the reading was clear. They waited. Her Le deluge was approaching. As with the actions of terrorists, one never knew around which corner one might meet death, or near death, mangling limbs, blindness.

Alex couldn't say she understood all of the emotions that made Celia do what she did; she may have had some love for him. The likely scenario is that her love, more than in most, was a love strongly configured to dependency, but peppered with genuine attraction and feelings of warmth. It would be an exaggeration to say that she loved him, to say it just like that, without qualification and psychological explanation. Given that, such a love, full of even understandable dependency, was very dangerous. The saving grace now was the fact that he had no delusions about Celia; Alex encouraged him to be strong on that point. She put it right out there. "You do realize, Gregory that you are diving into dangerous waters every time you talk to her? She is not responsible for what she does, but you can be terribly harmed nonetheless. You cannot help her problem. Walk away before it is too late."

Gregory understood. He had recovered. What he needed now was caution. His only concern now was keeping calm waters calm. "I'm fully aware of the dangers. However, I did hug her and kiss her on the cheek. I was unwise, and both of us are now paying the price. I need to get her stabilized before I leave her completely. I need to right the wrong I caused. Of course, perhaps I'm just being foolish. It's difficult to assess, rationally."

He was wrong, but he wanted to help. He did not realize and Alex could not convince him that, in this case, there was no cure. The disease had spread throughout the entire body.

Her entry of January 6, 1998

"Tonight I firmed up my decision to make one last attempt to make this man be a man. If I do not succeed, I shall retaliate in a serious manner for the humiliations he has heaped on me. I took a full day off work. He called yesterday and said he wanted to have a long chat, to settle once and for all whatever misunderstandings that remained between us. Naturally, I took that as a positive sign, a sign that he was going to own up to his irresponsible actions, his toying and playing with me. I am, after all, a grown, well-educated and serious woman. Finally, he appeared to be ready to do what I know is best for us. I was full of joy and hope. I asked, "Do you have a bit of time? This discussion is important. I can take the day off. We can chat, and perhaps take a drive somewhere and have lunch together."

He agreed. I don't worry about my husband because he no longer calls to check on me, or anything like that. He did when we first married, so one day I told him, "If you don't trust me I will leave this marriage." He never called me at work again, except for the day my father died. That, by the way, was a wonderful day for me. That bastard did not deserve to live. I had not seen him since I was eighteen. I hate him all the more because I can see my face in his image. I destroyed every photograph, but he still haunts me. My sexual life, I almost hate. I go from penis to penis, almost indiscriminately. He went from pussy to pussy, even mine, indiscriminately. I hate being him. I hate it. Oh God, I hate it. Gregory is the key to liberation. I'm on the altar. Some say, "You seem so natural there, next to the Blessed Sacrament. Made for you." Others say, "You are so quiet, so gentle, so solemn almost. You could have been, well, a nun. Yes, that's it, a nun, a modern one." No one sees the evil in me, my father in me: No one, not Alex, not Gregory, no one.

We met at a Holiday Inn in New Hampshire, about 70 miles from the Massachusetts border. As I drove along the hilly countryside I could glance down across the valley and see the blue tops of trees. A beautiful sight. What is grander than the self-confidence of a rugged mountain? Someone once said that the only creature not following God's Commands, is man. A bird will always act according to its nature. But man? Oh no. We're so damn smart, so prone to evil.

His first words when we entered the foyer, 'You look great! I hope you are feeling much better after your fainting event.'

I played with him. "Do you think I have animal magnetism, maybe?"

'Well, we are all animals, really.'

'So, I'm just an animal to you?'

He smiled. 'We are all part animal. The animal in us certainly brings grief at times.' He wore a wide grin. In his presence, the air texture changed to something casual, light, even giddy.

We brunched; naturally I assumed that the brunch would be a prelude to a final reconciliation; how would I think otherwise? After all, he called me an animal. What else could that mean except a tryst? He kissed me on the cheek, gave me a big hug. All of this, it seemed to me, was a prelude to further activity. Would you not have drawn a similar conclusion?

We were seated at a table that gave us a wonderful view of the gardens and tree groves that surrounded the hotel. The moment was enhanced by the rustling sound of wind-driven branches just outside the dining room window. They seemed to be crying out, 'Look at us, how beautiful we are.'

For me it was a magic moment; we had reached, it seemed at that moment, a new plateau of intimacy and sensuality. I became lost in a cloud, moving in and out of it, scarcely hearing what he was saying. Suddenly, the words, 'I am terribly sorry,' got through to me.

'Terribly sorry about what?' I asked in alarm.

'Haven't you been listening?'

The spell was broken. I sensed danger and a torrent of blood rushed to my head, causing sharp pains. I found myself trapped in steel, no way out. As his face moved across mine the low dining room light faded. He tried to be gentle, but it was too late. 'Celia, I am saying that this is the last time I am going to see you privately. I am here to apologize to you if in any gesture of mine gave you the wrong impression. That happens in life sometime, and if it happened here, even though not intended, I ask you to forgive me.'

I'm not clear about what happened next, but I recall tugging at his shirt, ripping it open, and feeling the warmth of his chest. I slapped him repeatedly and pulled at the clasp of his belt buckle. I wanted to rip it away from his waist and smash it against his face and chest and arms. My hands splayed against his ribs. I pulled at his chest hair. As if in a distance, I heard him calling my name. It was as if we were in the midst of a hurricane, with furniture and cutlery moving rapidly in and out of my vision. It was all fuzzy and powerful. He held me tight and carried me out to the parking lot, telling the maitre de 'She's having a spell. I will take care of it. It happens now and then.'

He kept hold of me but I finally broke free and ran to my car, as he shouted,   'Talk to me, for God's sake, say something.'

Talk to him! I'm going to do more than talk to him, the obscene bastard. This time I saw my father in his face."

Alex knew about the visit, indirectly, from a few remarks she made, but, otherwise, she was in the dark. Neither gave her any details. He simply said, "Well, I gave it another try, but she simply is on a different wave length, making a very big case out of a kiss on the cheek and a few hugs. I was stupid, of course."

She said, "That bastard needs to be punished for tearing at my life and then dumping me."

Alex's new life of liberation had already begun, but now, on the spot, she lied, but for a different reason than before. She needed to help her leave him for her sake. He was already saved. Alex had been saved. Now Celia needed to be saved. Alex pretended to sympathize. "You must feel terrible." Dread dragged at her psyche. It's a good thing her office was in her home because for at least a week he was incommunicado. His secretary would say, "I'm sorry, Father is down with some sort of a virus, but he will be fine by the weekend." The worst part was that he was not confiding in Alex; he was saying nothing at all. She was unable to leave the house. Where is there to go when your destination has relocated to somewhere unknown? He was not available. The wonderful times they had spent together in her home were put on hold. He called briefly to say that he was fine, that he needed time to be alone. That was clear. Thank God he had been liberated. Otherwise, Alex didn't know what she might have done to herself, to Celia, to him.

Celia began spending more time in her small cabin in the mountains. She had often invited her latest sex slave there for a tryst. She dignified it by calling it her love nest. Alex had access to it, if she wanted to, whenever Celia was not there. She was told where to find the key, hidden beneath the middle of three rocks lined up in a row. "The rocks are just beneath the outside water spigot."

Celia was there, alone. She easily received permission from her boss to take a few days off. It was the calm before the storm, but there was one more twist to our story that needs to be told, for fuller understanding.

CHAPTER TWENTY

Walter Shields had been hired by Celia's firm to help any employee who developed work-related stress. At the moment he was working on a troubled but key engineer in her department. Like most men, Shields was hot for her. She made the mistake of inviting him for lunch and, as he cleverly looked for a chink in her armor, lucked out when he said, "By the way, I've got a tiny problem of my own. What about some informal advice? It has to do with a female employee in another plant, and I would appreciate your feminine insights."

That got him four meetings in a row with her, alone. He knew what he wanted from her. He now had her, unsuspectingly, in a situation where sex and women would be discussed at length. Then he planned to intersect these conversations with how men think in the particular situation. To his utter amazement she was now so comfortable with this man who seemed to have all the answers that she did some confiding of her own. "I'm being sexually abused by a priest." Bingo! He won the lotto without purchasing a ticket, the Battle of Lexington without firing a shot. Copulation and copulation alone drenched his imagination. A thousand images at every angle in a room of a thousand mirrors skipped along the ridges of his brain. He knew exactly what to do, what buttons to press. He had, after all, been trained at Harvard University to do just that. More, he topped his class in results. His parents were proud of him; his professors lauded his bright future, the University was proud to claim him as their own, even inviting him to give prestigious lectures, well publicized in advance. He drew large audiences. He was a master of his profession. He would now practice his considerable talents and art until copulation. He looked at his handsome face in the mirror and declared. "She is mine."

Control is the name of the game. He immediately began to do what he accused the priest of doing, i.e., using his professional authority to intimidate, control, and titillate her. He knew, from his own expert knowledge, that he was hideous. He saw that, unequivocally, in the same mirror at which he proclaimed that she was his. It was, he convinced himself, this hideousness, looked at from the proper perspective, a perk of his profession. Everyone does it. Everyone uses the tools at hand. He was not, in the mind that he fashioned especially for this side of his personality, hideous, or anything like that. In fact, he devised a new tool just for her, his most potent herb, fright. He thoroughly frightened her. He worked at it so assiduously that before long he had her completely under his control. He told her that he would be her brother, that she could confide everything to him. He would then professionally interpret all she told him, thereby helping her. He even charged her a higher fee than normal. He was, in fact, not allowed to charge any employee a fee. He called it moonlighting and she never questioned his integrity. He was a snake in the grass, a manipulator par excellence, but she could not see it. It was ironic. Here was this great manipulator being manipulated. There are many such stories in the histories of great men. His experience had taught him that patient waiting for the right moment to strike was crucial; he would wait until she asked to be consoled.

He examined every nook and cranny of her sexual life, learning exactly what buttons to push and when. He would say, "I do not want o be intrusive, Celia, but in order to help you in this difficult and highly unusual case, I most know your most intimate thoughts about sexuality. Do you understand this? I need your explicit permission to probe so deeply. Do I have it? Feel free to say, no."

She was eager to heal." You have it, unconditionally. I trust you. You are a very good man. I thank God you came into my life. I will sign a paper, if want."
He wanted no paper trail on this one. "Not necessary. I take you on your word. You are sweet and you are trustworthy."

He was preparing himself to be her lover. He clinically discovered from conversations that what she really needed was someone to love her for whom she was. This became the key that would open every door for him. He told her how important it was that she have a true love in her life, one that was not just using her money for gambling, or taking advantage of the clerical collar to win her over, a man who really understood her. He was excited when she said, "You are the only man who understands me," thus fulfilling his prophecy. He was setting himself up as her Messiah and Savior, the only man who understood her, thus, logically, as he had prepared her, the man she must choose as her lover.

Her previous anxiety about wanting to sleep with a man who was also a priest now came back full blown under Walter's expert guidance. He explained that Gregory really did not love her, that his game was the control game. He wanted to play around with her, while remaining in the security of the priesthood. This tied-in with her previous accusation that Gregory just wanted to come and take what she had to offer, without accepting any responsibilities as a husband. Of course, Walter discovered that Jack gambled away her money. This allowed Walter to work on both fronts at once; i.e. Jack's irresponsibility and Gregory's manipulation. He was covering all the bases. He did not want her to go running back to Jack after he finished discrediting Gregory. He would bed her after obliterating all the competition.

Celia was listening to this guy like he was God Himself. She worshiped at his shrine. No praise was exaggeration. He deserved even more. She wanted Alex to meet him. "You must meet him. You simply must meet him. I insist."

She was very excited. "Come, join me for lunch at the plant tomorrow. You absolutely must meet him. He's incredible." She left a luncheon pass at the plant's front desk. Having been there a few times already, Alex was aware of the procedure. As she entered the large dining hall she spotted them immediately. Celia looked very cute in a white cotton blouse, a navy skirt and black moccasins. She was leaning toward him intently as they chatted, bathed in the bright illumination of dome lights. She formed a little steeple with her folded hands, leaning her chin on them as though in prayer. He was taking in her softened hair, inhaling her scent. Alex could almost hear the sound as he plucked her heartstrings. He was a man who knew how to chat up a woman; every profession has its artists. Celia looked over "Alex, right here. Come." Alex envied her unremarkable appearance, her tidy nose and unpainted lips.

He stood politely, and with a slight courtesan bow of the head, "I'm so happy to meet you. Celia has told me all about you, and what a great friend you are. She is so lucky."

In spite of his warm brown eyes, square chin and tumbling

black hair that drooped over his forehead, all Alex could think about was snake oil. A thin scar meandered like a piece of thread across the lower right hand side of his jaw. He held a chair and she sat down. The chair's movement echoed off the dining room cement floor, like an omen. She could feel the clever undercurrents of thought swirling about his head. He suddenly leaned over, whispered something into her ear, and laughed. Turning to Alex he said, "I'm sorry. How rude of me. But, I just couldn't resist this private joke. Celia is such a good sport."

After exchanging pleasantries she ventured, "Oh, where did you study?"

He laughed. "I grew up in Boston, in the streets of America. I finished two years at U Mass in Economics, and then realized that my vocation was in helping people. I switched to psychology, got my Masters at Harvard, and hung out my shingle. Counseling is such rewarding work."

Celia beamed with pride at her discovery. "Isn't that marvelous? Harvard, no less! Walter has helped me so much." One aspect of her growing dependence on this guy was a softening, more feminine face. It was all so strange.

For his part, he brazenly eyed her as a nice plump dessert to be swallowed after the main course.

"Are you married?" Alex asked.

"I used to be. She was a nice girl but was tied to her mother and really wasn't prepared to take on a husband."

'And you were not easy to live with!'

He continued, looking directly at Celia, "I'm just waiting for the right girl to come along. Someone like your friend Celia here!"

Alex felt a hard knot of distress tighten in her stomach, and her cheeks flushed red with distress. Was he smooth or what? She tried to shake away the disturbing image of a circus barker, but it persisted. The only consolation was the hope that he would take her away from Gregory. Walter could become Gregory's unwitting savior. What twists and turns our meandering lives take. On the one hand Alex knew this was an unkind thought, but she seemed to be, as men say, asking for trouble. Walter certainly was no solution to her intractable problem, but Alex knew there was no way of persuading her otherwise.

A few days later Celia came over to Alex's place during her
lunch hour. The weather was bad. She drove alongside the curb,
as usual, with her engine roaring and slamming of brakes. She
always drove like this when she was excited. She met raining
sleet that the bitter wind had turned into stinging droplets of ice.
Celia popped open an umbrella as she pushed the car door open
with her feet, and hurried up the sidewalk to the house, tossing a
lingering look at her car, afraid the sleet might damage it. Her
face reddened in the elements. She rang the doorbell furiously, as
if Alex was refusing to answer. Alex opened the door as quickly
as she could. She rushed to stand in front of the living room
mirror, checking her appearance. Alex got her settled down in the
living room. She sank into one of the chairs and asked, hurriedly,
"What do you think of him?"

"Who?"

"Walter, of course, dummy. How many men do you think I
have?" With a giggle, "Don't answer that question. Tell me. Isn't
he great?"

Alex hesitated. Celia placed her hands together, digging her
nails into them. Glancing at her apprehensively, she lowered her
brow in a mild scowl. "Tell me! What do you think of him?" In
misreading him, she, the predator, was on the verge of becoming
the victim. Many of Alex's patients suffer from this problem.
She cranked up the courage. "He did not impress me. He's bit
too smooth for my taste. I may be wrong."

"Oh, Alex, you are," was her succinct reply, but said without
anger or resentment. She was now right back full circle to getting
herself into another sexual relationship that would go nowhere.
She had the perverse virtue of being attracted to men for the
wrong reasons, and now she had a man who was attracted to her
for the wrong reasons. This was her curse.
That she was headed for trouble was also indicated by the fact
that instead of having pulled her hair back to a simple ponytail,
she had taken the time to blow-dry it so that it fell on her
shoulders. She was on the prowl. Celia was a silent woman who
talked with body language, eloquently; a mistress of the art of
the soft understatement, the subtle, as men who became
entangled into her well-woven web discovered. At this moment,
on the verge of being bedded by her therapist, she was ready to

explode.

Alex needed an answer to the sixty-four dollar question. "What does he say about Gregory?"

The answer poured out. "He made it clearer to me than ever before what an abusive, evil and manipulative priest he is. I'm going to report him to the archbishop so that he will not continue to harm other women."

Alex felt a twinge of the same anger that swelled up in her every time she made negative references to a man she had entrapped, and prepared to destroy. Her heart sank. How could this Black Widow of a woman destroy this good man? She knew she had to act. "Celia, please, let it be. Whatever his weaknesses are, he is not an evil man. He is a good man who became very attracted to you. Please don't do this to him. Anyway, if you do, Jack is going to find out about it and that won't help your situation any. Also, Gregory is very honest. He is not going to deny that he flirted with you and might also describe, if grilled by the authorities, your own actions. This means your reputation in this town will be finished and you might have to leave your company just as you had to leave McDonnell-Douglas. Please don't cause all that destruction. I promise you I will speak to him and get him to understand how much harm he did. Give him a break. After all, he may have flirted but when he had a chance to be intimate with you he did not take advantage of you. Please."

Her eyes opened wide when Alex said her reputation would be destroyed in the firestorm that would follow such a revelation. She slapped her leg and shouted, "Damn, I didn't thank of that! Of course, Gregory will tell it all. That's the way he is. Oh, my God, I'd better tell Walter I'm not going to do that."

Alex acted surprised, "Walter? This is Walter's idea?" She grabbed her by the shoulders. "Celia, be careful of his advice. My God, that doesn't make sense. You would think that he would be wiser than that."

She gasped and said, "You're right. Well, I guess he was just telling me the technically correct thing to do. I guess. I mean, yeah, that was a dumb suggestion. I'd better tell Walter to be more practical from now on."

Gregory held her spellbound, and she felt trapped. His tenderness and generosity of spirit lay beyond the ken of her understanding. But there was a shift of intent. It was becoming obvious that he no longer was a bit of sport for her, something to while away her time. This was heavy. Falling in love? That possibility was real. And, here was this scam artist holding her in the palm of his hands, absorbed in studying how to manipulate her. Alex wondered if she would really change her mind about going to the archbishop. She knew one thing: she would be waiting in the lobby of his office to see him as soon as she came out.

Given his determination to avoid her, the dangers were now multiplying exponentially. "Well, Celia, do what you feel you must do, but you know I don't agree that he's a bad person. He's just another human being like you and me."

She hesitated. "Well, I'll think about that."

CHAPTER TWENTY ONE

Her diary entry of Valentine's Day told me, in a general way at least, what she did:

I got Gregory on the phone today, Valentine's Day. 'You said we would not be meeting again privately. Does that include phone calls?' He was cleverly soft. 'Of course not; call me any time. I hope you are feeling better.'

That was all this creep had to say about dumping me in public in the dining room of a hotel? I let him ramble on. When he ran out of steam, I simply said. 'You are a real son-of-a-bitch. You are a corrupt and manipulative person. You used your collar, to collar women, irresponsibly. I hate you and everything you stand for. I think you should be destroyed, thrown out of the Church and ground underneath the feet of all Catholics. If Jack would not get hurt so badly, I would expose you. If you ever call me again, I will report you to the police for sexual harassment.' Then I just hung up on him and instructed my secretary not to accept any calls for me that day because I was working on a special project. But, I must have scared the shit out of him because he did not call. I have finally and definitively gotten rid of the bastard. I feel so much cleaner about myself now.

In her diary Alex found a letter he sent to her shortly after that phone call. Her heart went out to him.

Celia:

Your phone call has stunned me. Am I a priest who engaged in some innocent flirting with you? Yes, I am. I have explained to you that in my honest opinion the vow of chastity, number one, is violated frequently, and that the vow of celibacy causes so many other problems, (alcoholism, the obsession with material things, extreme loneliness, etc,) that it should be abolished. However, my choice is simple. I remain a priest and keep my vows, or I leave and get married. My choice is to remain. If you wish to report me to the Archdiocese, I cannot stop you. I do think, however, considering your very open challenge to me to go further with you, that you are not being fair.

As regards manipulating you--let me give you a different scenario, the one that I experienced. I will try to be brutally honest, not trying to cover up my own faults. Our closeness began, first of all, because one day while we were shopping in Hyde Park, you suddenly put your arms around me, and kissed me full on the lips. That beginning, at least, can hardly be described as manipulation on my part. I was always the cautious person who moved so slowly that on many occasions you complained that I was manipulating you because I did not do more. Please reflect on the series of events and encounters. Perhaps that might give you a different perspective on our relationship.

I am also asking that you reflect on the harshness of the language you used in our telephone call. From my perspective, and knowing a lot about your past (from your own lips), is there a chance that you might be trying to cover up your own failings? Think about it. In any case, I thank you for the time you gave me and I regret that our relationship ended in such a manner. I tried mightily not to make it end so. You know I wish you well.

God Bless,

Gregory

Alex thought Gregory's letter well written and reflecting the true nature of the relationship. She thought his reply made a huge impact on Celia because, except for a brief "I got a letter from him distorting everything that happened between us" she was very quiet about him. Alex kept the letter for evidence, if needed. The next Parish Council meeting took place only ten days after the receipt of this letter. Celia attended the meeting, saying, "He's out of town, so I'll show up." After the meeting she suggested that they go for a pizza. They spent a good two hours talking about parish and other business, but she never mentioned his name once. Alex thought she appeared very, very sad, her words not coming out of her mouth lightly. Her body movements were labored. Alex knew the feeling. She knew that when she was sad it slowed up her whole psyche, making her body a ton weight. During those two hours, Celia frequently stared into space. Alex could only believe that she was thinking of him. She had a premonition that something bad was about to happen, and it did.

The very next morning Alex got a call from Jack. "Celia has tried to commit suicide. Please come quickly." His voice was highly nervous and he hung up. She rushed over to the house and arrived just as Emergency Services was loading her into an ambulance. The very sight of whirling red and blue lights was itself a fright. She often thought that one day she would be in one of those vehicles for some reason or another. Ambulances always distressed her, reminding her of her mortality. The medics allowed her a moment to try and talk with Celia but her eyes remained closed. Alex put a trembling Jack into the passenger seat of her car, and they followed the ambulance to the hospital. Apparently she had swallowed too many barbiturates. Within hours of her entry into the hospital, Alex was able to visit her. She spoke quietly, waiting until Jack left before she opened up. Whether she intended just to ease her pain or she had more in mind was not clear. What she did say was, "Even though he's a bastard, I'm having a tough time losing Gregory. I just needed something to knock me out."

Alex thought it significant that Walter, the therapist, was not by her side. "Where is Walter? Don't you need his help right now?"

She sat in the chair next to the bed, her legs drawn up tightly against her breast and a defiant jutting forth of her chin. "He's the guy who got me into this state, so I don't want to see him right now, even if his theory is correct."

"What theory?"

"The theory that Gregory is using the power and authority of his priesthood to manipulate me." She shifted her legs, cross-legging them beneath her, and her eyes sparkled with diamond-hard tears. Obviously, Gregory, at least for the moment, was now becoming much less the demon that she had portrayed him to be. There was at least a temporary backing off of placing full responsibility on his shoulders.

Alex encouraged her in this. "Well, Celia, no matter what Gregory's intentions were, you have to admit that you did encourage him. No woman your age and with your education (she wanted to say 'experience' but thought the connotation too harsh in this environment) can use as an excuse that she is being totally hoodwinked. Besides, can you really say that Gregory is a con artist? Nothing else he has done in the parish indicates that he is such a man. If anything, he has risked a lot by being so open about himself, he said publicly that he envied people who were in a good marriage, that the life of a priest is terribly lonely."

Resting her chin on a fist and with an indignant raising of her shoulders, she simply said, "Well, this isn't the best time and the right setting to point that out to me. You should know better than to complicate matters in a hospital setting. Shame on you." Then, with concern, "Did you notify Gregory?"

"No. Do you want me to? The way you've been talking about him that would never even occur to me."

Irritated, "Of course I want you to call him. I mean, for God's sake, can't you see the condition I'm in?" Sharply, "Doesn't that make a difference? I don't want him to go traipsing off somewhere not knowing that I'm in the hospital."

Alex simply said. "Ah, of course, it does."

"Thanks for being sensible. My God, common sense is the most difficult thing to find these days."

Alex guessed she was being complimented, so she said, "Thanks."

She looked at me, "Well?" clearly meaning that I should call him right there and then.

"I'm off to find a telephone. I'll do it right now"

"Find a telephone? There is one right here!"

Celia had Alex in such a nervous state that she had not noticed the phone on the cabinet next to her bed. "What should I tell him?"

She placed her forefinger to her cheek, and thought for a bit. "First of all, tell him I am very sick in the hospital. I just want to see what he will do."

"And, if he asks what is wrong?"

She did not hesitate. "Tell him I took an overdose because I was distraught."

"Should I say about what?"

"No, let him ask. If he's interested he will ask."

"Fine." Alex quickly dialed and he answered. "Gregory, Celia is quite sick. I am with her here in the hospital. I thought you should know."

The concern was in his tone of voice. "What happened?"

"She took an overdose of something."

"What brought that about?"

"I asked her and she said she was distraught."

"Over what?"

"I asked her but she didn't say."

"Well, I'm awfully sorry to hear that. Give her my best wishes and tell her that I hope she makes a quick recovery."

Alex asked him to hold for a moment because he was winding down the conversation and she wanted to let her know that. He evidently seemed uninterested in talking to her. Alex covered the phone with her hands. "Gregory sends his best wishes and hopes for a speedy recovery."

She was angry. "That's all! Didn't he say he would come over, or at least ask if he could come here to see me?"

"No, he didn't."

"That son of a bitch. Just hang up."

That Alex did not do. "Gregory. OK, sorry I interrupted you. Is there anything else you wanted to say before we hang up?"

He was cold. "No, not really."

With that, the conversation ended. Celia reached out for the phone just in time to hear its final soft click, then turned her face to the wall and pulled the covers over her head, saying. "I think you'd better go now. I don't feel like talking. He has no right to treat me this way."

CHAPTER TWENTY TWO

Once again, Celia was back to her old tricks. She blamed Gregory for a situation that she had created. She told him never to talk to her again. Alex left the hospital with mixed feelings. Two things had happened in that room. First of all, Celia was on the prowl for him again. There was no doubt about it. She could not really keep away from him. Secondly, he seemed far less interested in speaking with her than ever before. Alex had some hope, once again, that her time had come, but for reasons other than previously. They now had this wonderful relationship. Alex harbored a fear that Celia could spoil it all. She headed for a telephone booth and called him. "Since I really could not speak freely in front of Celia, how would you like to meet me at my house and I'll fill you in."

"Great idea. I can be at your place in about an hour."

Her heart skipped its usual beat whenever she talked to him. "Fine." She could not wait to hear his reaction to all of this.

Alex quickly mixed a bit of pasta with marinara sauce. She knew it would make no difference if he had already eaten. A small dish of pasta was something he never failed to dispose of quickly.

She got to know the sound of his car, so she raced to the door when she heard him pull into the driveway. He smiled as he walked quickly along the walkway to her door, looking great in a bulky gray sweater, with a woolen scarf wrapped around his neck He paused momentarily and glanced at the silver-spindled branches of my myrtle bush. "Hi. I'm hungry. Got something for a sandwich?"

As he walked through the door Alex put her arms around him and gave him a big hug. "Better than that. Pasta with *marinara* sauce."

He clenched his fist and thrust it into the air, something he did when expressing joy. Alex was no longer loaded with the tension of not knowing what he was going to decide to do about Celia. So, as they sat down to eat, almost casually, the words just came tumbling out of her mouth. "Are you going to contact Celia?" Previously, she would have asked this question after an agonizing tension and uncertainty. Freedom was so sweet.

Raising his eyes to the top of her head with a wide smile that spoke equanimity, he shrugged his shoulders and leaned back, stretched out his arms and, linking his fingers behind his head, said quietly, but firmly. "No. I don't think it's in the best interest of either of us." His eyes held a steadiness that reached beyond pity for Celia. It was so comforting.

"I'm sure that you already figured out that her taking all those barbiturates had something to do with you? Right?"

He lowered his head in sadness. "It did cross my mind. That is all the more reason to stop our relationship. It can't go anywhere. She is getting increasingly erratic and it can only end in some sort of dead end."

There was finality to his voice that Alex had not noticed previously. She ventured, "You know that I have a horse in this race, so to speak, but I really do agree with you. In my opinion, she is desperate for love but highly suspicious that it can come from you or anyone else. That damn therapist has poisoned an already suspicious mind. I wonder what the hell he plans to do now that she has broken his rules and made an attempt to get you back into her life?"

He paused a bit and said, "Well, whatever it is he plans to do she won't benefit from it. He's going to be increasingly furious that he has not succeeded in fully brainwashing her as yet. He, she, each of them or both of them could get even more dangerous. That's my take on it. But, I'm out of this now, unless I saw him with a gun in his hand aiming at her. In that case I'd try to prevent a tragedy."

He walked over to the bay window and looked out at her garden. The phone rang. It was Celia, sounding desperate again. "Alex, please call him and ask him to come and see me. I need to see him. I was foolish listening to that damn Walter. I think he wants to have his way with me. His therapy bullshit is just that, bullshit. Gregory is something solid. Please, Alex, help me. Ask him to call me."

She hung up before Alex could answer. Gregory guessed correctly. "Celia? Wants me to call?"

"Yes. Sorry, but a call would start you back on the road to nowhere."

Of course, Alex did not feel sorry. "You are doing the right thing. Certainly, you need time at least to think about it." She did not want to appear too eager. After all, her guess was, at the time, that he still cared for her in some way but saw the dangers and the uselessness of it all. The phone rang. Alex knew who it was. "Yes, Celia, what can I do for you?"

"You tell that Gregory I'm very serious this time. He can't just let me hang out to dry as if I'm some useless old rag." Try as she did to sound cold and forbidding, she could not hide the pain and confusion that she was experiencing.

Alex got bold. "But, Celia, you told him never to call you again. You told him it was all over. What in the name of heaven do you expect from him now?"

She softened, in a kind of exhausted way. "Yes, I know. Please, Alex, call him. Tell him I need to talk to him. Tell him I'm going crazy. Tell him anything. Just get him to call me, please!"

Alex did not give in, but was soft. "I will try, Celia. You know I cannot promise anything. Right?"

Resigned. "Yes, I know. Please try, that's all I ask."

Alex told Gregory what she said, even the part about her going to the Archbishop. He replied that he almost wished she would get that over with and simply go down to the Archdiocesan office and spill her guts. He really did not give a damn. He would only regret that she would portray a skewed picture of what had actually taken place. He was very calm, the calmness of a man who had long ago accepted that something was inevitable. "I've known for a long time that this is how it would turn out."

Alex thought it was in his best interest and therefore, in the long term, her best interest, if he no longer gave in to her demands. He evidently held the same opinion. In the past she would get to him and he would yield. This time it appeared he would not. He was not interested in her threats, no longer held hostage. He saw how egocentric she was and what damage she might do if her wishes were not fulfilled. That's exactly what happened.

CHAPTER TWENTY THREE

At this point Walter came back into the picture. From an eyewitness account, Celia's secretary, and what Celia later told me, Alex pieced together this account of what happened. Using his official title as Company therapist he entered the high security area where Celia worked, entered her office, told the secretary to leave and closed the office door before Celia had a chance to react. He carried a threatening glint in his eyes, and nervously rubbed the back of his neck. She gestured helplessly. She could have physically left but was frozen in her chair by the fierceness in his glaring eyes. He menacingly traced one finger along her cheek and under her eyelids. He spoke softly so as not to attract the attention of the other employees, but his words were harsh. He accused her of demeaning his professional ability by telling some of her friends that he had been a hindrance rather than a help to her. He accused her of leading him on, romantically telling him that she had finally found someone she could count on and that he would make a wonderful life partner. He said he heard through the grapevine (who turned out to be a girlfriend of the parish secretary) that she had called Gregory, against his professional advice, thereby undermining her trust in him and his trust in her.

She murmured a soft protest but became silent when this provoked even more danger. She later described him as appearing extremely restless and flushed, as with a fever. For a man who boasted that he never allowed himself to lose control, no matter what the provocation, who said that calmness and reasonableness were essential ingredients in the mix that helped his patients, he had lost it. She felt the heat of the seething emanating from his pores and body language. She suggested that they go out for lunch somewhere. He agreed.

They stopped off at Luigi's Italian Restaurant for some salad and pasta. During the course of the conversation he became visibly enraged, swept both meals off the table and slapped her in the face. She screamed for help and a waiter flagged down a police car. Walter was arrested for destruction of restaurant property and battery. It made the newspapers. Jack had had enough. He moved out into the small bungalow of a girlfriend, about twenty miles away, called his lawyer and initiated divorce proceedings. Since they held all of their property in common and since she did not contest the divorce he did not include the house in the settlement, giving her shelter and part of the little money left after his gambling sprees. At work, the President of the company called Celia to his office. He warned her that any such further public behavior or hospitalization for emotional reasons could result in the elimination of her job. Her life was now in shambles.

Gregory remained aloof. Alex urged him to call Celia and wish her well, but he refused. In his eyes, she could see the pain and turmoil, the blame he poured on himself, but there was no visible act of consolation from Gregory, not even a phone call.

One late afternoon Celia showed up at Alex's house wearing a beige cotton-knit sweater, pulled down low over her patchy jeans. She tried to say a few words but her voice broke, revealing her suffering. It brought tears to Alex's eyes. Another vision, almost an alien vision of her was staring at Alex through bloodshot eyes. She gripped her handbag so tightly that her knuckles turned white. Alex thought her skeletal parts might emerge from her skin at any moment. Sighing heavily, she plunked herself down on the living room carpet, covered herself with a ruffled blue coverlet lying folded on the couch, and dramatically clasped her hands behind her head. Her fingers nervously traced the contours of her face. Alex put a pillow behind her head. She remained there until late evening, getting up only to use the bathroom. Alex could not convince her to use the guest bedroom. As she watched her pliant lips softly expelling her sleeping breath, Alex had to acknowledge, once again, the sensuousness of her beauty, a beauty that had little external beauty! Didn't make sense, but there it was, clear as a bell.

The one consolation Alex had was that Celia no longer spoke with whimsical self-satisfaction and self-confidence. The fight had gone out of her. She spoke of retreating to Italy, somewhere along the Amalfi coast where she had seen small but cozy stone houses surrounded by aromatic pines and olive trees, along the seashore's rim. This could entice Gregory, she said, and they could live happy and romantic lives forever. Surely, she said, she could manage to buy one. They could live and die in Gregory's ancestral homeland.

Sometime around midnight Alex handed her a couple of sandwiches. She sat up to eat and they resumed chatting; they talked most of the night. It was all about Gregory. Moments of accusations and moments of praise and admiration intersected each other. Finally, she fell asleep on the soft and fluffy couch. Alex was afraid she might have some barbiturates in her purse that she could swallow during the night, so she examined the purse, finding nothing that could do her harm. Walter was in jail; Gregory was incommunicado. Jack had left her. Her job was in jeopardy. She retreated to the world of fantasy. Alex checked on her several times. There she was, broken, but shining through the night.

The next morning, as soon as the dawn light flooded the room, she uncurled herself from the sofa, her hair swinging behind her as she rose. As unkempt as it was, it looked soft and supple. Before she left, she took one last look at herself in the long mirror on the bathroom door. "Horrible," she murmured, as she fingered and tossed her hair. After a quick shower, she got back into her pantsuit and did something she rarely did, applied a bit of makeup. With a "Pray for me," she went off to work with ruffled hair, glassy eyes and increasingly shrunken cheeks. She was now rapidly becoming wan and fragile, a caricature of her former self.

CHAPTER TWENTY FOUR

Celia, who used to call Alex perhaps once or twice a week, now called several times a day, harboring such intense emotions as to continually raise her anxiety level. She sounded alternately clear, then confused, saying "Oh," as she readjusted her thinking every few moments. She even called Jack and asked if he would come and watch TV with her. He agreed. She confided in him the entire messy story. His reaction to her outpouring surprised her. "I knew all about it, not in detail, but that you were crazy about him. Remember, we've lived together for many years. I know who you are, not all of you, of course, no one does. But, I know both what you need and the fact that I cannot provide it for you. So, I understood."

A friend informed him that he had seen both of them together two or three times, and each time they appeared to be absorbed in each other. That, of course, was an exaggeration, but good gossip. Jack had picked up bits and pieces of her infidelities, going back for years. "How did this affect you?"

"I stopped loving you years ago. I guess I was too comfortable in our home and I had no special romantic interest, so I just stayed. There's a girl I've been seeing but I don't know if it is going to lead to anything. I'm staying at her house. I see her mostly for sex and companionship. You are welcome to her place anytime you wish to visit."

Celia said, "I don't know why, but I was infuriated that he was seeing another girl. I just slammed the phone down as if it had snapped at me." She paused to take a breath and added, "Of course, if he has a new cash cow for his gambling orgies, that will make me one very happy lady, believe me." Once again she was balancing contradictions.

Alex did not mind her calls, but she did tense involuntarily whenever she heard her voice, like ominous clouds rolling in off the plains, like lethally glazed roads of black ice in a wintry morning rush hour. She pitied her because she could not bear to have the illusionary veils of awesome power torn away from her psyche. Her last hope was Gregory. This is what constituted the greatest danger, her need for him. Gone were the days when she would simply go on the prowl, satisfy and be satisfied her proven and, let's face it, undeniable sexual prowess became her last vestige of hope. "He can't possibly be that much different from other men."

She later learned that Jack's new girlfriend was indeed his new gambling cash cow. In any case, she got some comfort from his visits. It was being with someone familiar that helped her in her loneliness. Jack informed her, "My girlfriend does not mind if I visit you. She's very understanding."

Celia continued to press Alex to broker a new meeting with Gregory. She told her the truth this time because she did not want to endanger my own position, and the truth was helpful to Alex. "He told me, Celia, that under no condition does he want to resume the relationship."

Alex brought her some soup. There she was, sitting in the worn and well-padded rocking chair she loved so much, staring out at the horizon, a white coverlet wrapped around her, the kind they throw over dead bodies. Alex had no doubt that she was absorbed in thoughts of Gregory. "Alex, I could go to Mass and see him there, but it's all so hurtful. To see him now as a stranger, as someone who does not want to talk to me. That would be horrific, much better if we had never met. I spend my days alternating between rage and fits of crying. I have a hell of a problem severing ties, even those that are bad for me. At night I wrap my legs around this long body pillow and imagine all sorts of couplings. My existence is no existence at all."

Alex knew when she was leaning into the phone. She could hear her inhaling and exhaling breath clearly; she was suffocating internally and it took its toll externally, like having carried a large weight up a flight of stairs. Sheer exhaustion and enervation were now part of her hourly existence. Alex gnawed at her thumbnails while waiting to speak. She could image the dimple on the left side of her mouth quivering. She felt the urge to express the first tentative seeds of her own independent thought and say something she had wanted to say for a long time. "Well, Celia, you have this consolation, that he never considered you just for sex. If he did, he would have taken advantage of you long ago. He would be with you right now. With Jack out of the house he could have a ball with you, if that is what he was after."

She interrupted the flow of our conversation by making reference to the blossoming of spring tulips, daffodils, and tiny little green leaves that were beginning to appear on the trees. Then, she returned to her subject. "Oh God, I know. I've thought about that a hundred times. I was such a fool. I destroyed the only good thing that has happened to me in years. What a fool I have been! For days I've felt like I've had an operation without anesthesia. I try to ignore this tug of my heart but I can't."

She paused for the span of a musical note, then continued. "I'm haunted by his eyes and his gentleness. When he is laughing, his eyes look deeper into me than at other times. When he concentrates on me like that I feel weak. I even think of him with his hands in the pockets of the light woolen slacks he wears sometimes, and the plaid jacket he treasures so much. He always looks as unkempt as a philosophy professor, but his speech is as precise as an economics professor and as sweet as a poem. An entire film of him flits across my mind's eye in an instant. I've never been so sad in my entire life. By my own actions I lost what was left of beauty and integrity in my life. Sometimes I see red, trickles of blood washing over my eyes. I live in a murky mix of sanity and depression. He can survive because he is accustomed to deprivation. I can't"

She made a sound like that of grinding teeth. She seemed both to be pouting at herself and engaging in a pellucid analysis of her situation and how she got there. Her mood was that of tension-charged stillness, a mood she had cultivated over the years. At the same time Alex sensed that she was preparing herself for action. In some, this juxtaposition would not be logical, but in her it was fitting. The lion reflects beauty as it crouches, silently, readying itself to leap. Yet, she would have to conclude that 'bizarre' was also an accurate description of Celia's behavior.

Just listening to her was a bruising experience. Even if she were capable of putting behind her the loss, the bleeding scars would remain forever; reminders always of what she, in her flood of self-pity, could only define as abuse and betrayal. A sudden, inoperable disease would have been a blessed event for her. And yet Alex's resentment of her continued to lay, like blood, just under her skin.

As she talked, Alex could feel the warmth of the blinding sun through the living room bay windows. Spring was approaching New England. The muted sound of traffic brought her to trip dreaming. She had a momentary image of walking hand in hand with Gregory along some sun-kissed stretch of seashore, foamy waves pounding their way towards them, catching their ankles in a caress. There was in him a kind of sensual restlessness born of the need to know more, to conquer difficult problems, or organize a fruitful project. His intuitiveness was complimented by a no-nonsense practicality, a nice combination.

She looked out at her chrysanthemums, splashes of pink and yellow. How wonderful to be a flower. Perhaps they are lucky not to be conscious of their blessed condition. If they were, would they not be proud, thus spoiling the image we have of them? They dumbly but gloriously reflect God's goodness and beauty.

When Celia got off the phone Alex relaxed with a glass of wine. Then she downed a second glass. That gave her the good old alcoholic glow, an enticing lassitude throughout her body. She pushed a Celine Dionne tape into the tape deck, curled up on her couch with soft fluffy pink pillows, and imagined Gregory putting his arms around her, his face flush with hers, his hot breath showering her with sensual warmth. As she downed the remainder of her wine, she luxuriated in the truth suggested by Hamlet: This above all: to thine own self be true. Her truth was that she wanted to live with Gregory. If he ever asked for that she would run to him.

Alex built a fire in the fireplace and listened to the comforting sounds of hissing gas flowing out from cracks in the burning logs. She wrapped a light blanket around herself imagining his arms holding her in warmth and security. Later that night she used her guest room for sleeping, a cute bedroom tucked away beneath the gables. It is small and very romantic. That's the kind of mood Alex was in. An artist fiend who loved ocean views, said, "I'm leaving my easel here, so I can take up where I left off." From that room one has a clear view of the harbor spotted with sail boats in slight floating motion, bedecked with a bevy of multi-striped flags.

CHAPTER TWENTY FIVE

The alarm clock is permanently set for 6:45 AM. It's one of those real clingy things that force you to get up just to stop the awful noise. Alex shoved an extra pillow beneath her head, folded her arms, and simply meditated, looking out at the harbor and clear blue sky, thanking God for life and health. It was peaceful. The radio came blaring on with the morning news. "It has been reported that Father Gregory, popular pastor of St. John's Catholic Church, has been murdered in what the police believe a botched robbery attempt. Father Gregory Palermo was found slumped over his desk, where he had evidently been counting money. The safe was open. Except for a few dollar bills scattered on the desk, some of them drenched in his blood, no other money was found. Police have not as yet released any further information, other than to say that no weapon was found at the scene."

Alex was cornered; her back was against the wall; no route of escape, as the floodwaters of this news came tumbling towards her, engulfing her. She floundered in the inflexible grip of a monster storm, clawing fruitlessly against its force. Reproach overshadowed her for the failure to divine the obvious, to have been overcautious at a time when boldness was called for. She was a disaster caught in a disaster. She had set herself a target she could never achieve. She had found a resting place in her imagination, while outside the storm had already gathered and was, imminently, threatening to engulf the three of them. Alex waited to hear from Celia. There was no doubt whatsoever in hery mind that she was the assassin. He was gone and at this moment Alex's grief had to share mental space with her need not to become publicly associated with any of this. For the first time in many months she focused on self-preservation. She would like to think that is normal, not cowardly; natural, not paranoid.

Alex went through her house gathering the casual clothing he left to use during his visits. She was torn between venerating them as relics and removing them as evidence of association. A computer carton served as the reliquary. Trousers, shirts, two pair of sandals, a Gillette razor, shaving cream, cologne, sport socks, an electric toothbrush, toothpaste, a spare watch, thirteen floppy disks containing information about meetings, some sermons and addresses. She taped the carton, writing on it, 'personal items, do not disturb.' Later, she raced downstairs, put the carton in her car, along with some kerosene, and drove off to the dump. She couldn't take the pressure. Two vagrants were the only persons at the dump when she arrived. They offered to take the carton. Alex waved them off, sat in her car until they drifted to another spot further along the way, poured the kerosene on the carton, and tossed a match that ignited swiftly and flashing large yellow flames that consumed everything. She removed a small snow shovel that was kept in the trunk of the car and feverishly spread the ashes along a fifteen or twenty foot circle. She then reached into the glove compartment of her car, seized her camera and was about to capture the ashy remains; but she changed her mind. Some scenes demand the poetry that only an artist could capture. A dump truck arriving as she left was the only visitor. As she turned the last curve out of the dump, she glanced down and observed that the wind was already scattering the ashes without reference to direction. It was all over.

Alex worked at home, so there was no one to report her missing at work. She wondered about Celia's situation. She was a vital part of the daily operations at the plant, adjusting the machinery, and replacing parts. She would certainly be missed. Alex waited three days before she emerged from her nest. She needed to know something, anything, so she passed by the plant's parking lot. Celia's space was empty. She checked again two hours later and the car was not there. She returned after another two hours; still vacant. Alex began to feel threatened. Was Celia watching her? Was she following her? Why did she not call? She had to know that Alex knew. She went to a public telephone and dialed her office. Teresa, her secretary, was very bland and unruffled. "Oh, Celia left a week ago on vacation. She has another week. Would you like to leave a message?"

"No, thanks. I will call after she returns. Thank you."

Obviously, all at the plant was normal. She planned well so that the dastardly deed be done 'while I was away.' But, why didn't she call? Then Alex remembered. Her vacation cabin did not have a phone. Jack, in the early days of their marriage had insisted. "No work away from work." Then it occurred to Alex that Jack had not called either. But then, he never called her except when Celia was sick. So, she had to assume that all was normal there also. Could she be wrong? Was it possible that Celia had not killed Gregory? No, it was not, because Jack would almost certainly have notified her about the murder, and Celia would have called. Or, he would have called Alex before or after calling Celia. The uncertainty of it all unsettled her.

Alex lived in tense anticipation for another three days. Then, she called. "Oh, my God, Alex, Jack got word to me up here and told me about Gregory. You know we have no phone and no TV here. I'm calling from the gas station. Please come. We need to talk. I'm devastated."

So, Jack was able to notify her in that remote region, but did not call Alex or pass by here? Not a likely scenario. Not at all likely. She tested the waters. "I will see you at the funeral and we can meet later."

"Alex, for God's sake, I couldn't bear being at the funeral. I might lose control. What would people think? Too risky."

Both of us had shifted into self-preservation gear. Alex understood.

"Take some medication. Keep yourself as calm as you can under the circumstances."

"And, for God's sake, Alex, don't tell anyone that I know about the murder and the funeral. If I do not come and they ask, just say 'I think she's up at her cabin-no phone, no television.' This way, if I don't show up, no one will criticize me later. Who knows, in their investigations the police will follow any leads, like who hung out with him and all that. Both of us have to be careful."

Her voice was different. Alex's mind's eye painted a picture of her surroundings. There would be no bookcases, no ornaments, no hint of softness. She had so failed to decorate the cabin that the only beauty her sex slaves would find there would be her welcoming arms and body, inviting, teasing. There she was, at the moment, sitting, covered with starkness, a murderess, calculating the avoidance of punishment. She was both a sexual nymph and an engineer, but the engineer in her was, in this crisis, dominant. She had a strategy. Alex knew her well enough to conclude that she, being the only one, other than Jack, who could suspect or even be convinced of her guilt, had to be very cautious. It was scary.

The parish mourned the death of a well-loved priest. One would have to be a Catholic to know how deep those feelings go. Alex kept a low profile as preparations for his funeral proceeded. Council met and passed a resolution to memorialize his passing in a manner to be determined at a later date. Some suggested it fitting to establish a scholarship to one of the top universities, like Harvard, or Yale, or Princeton, since he was, as far as anyone present could recall, the only priest intellectual ever to serve as pastor in the parish's recent history. They also passed another resolution calling on local police authorities to pursue with all vigor the identity of the killer. In the letter to the Commissioner of Police, they noted that "the murder of a priest is a destabilizing act, an affront to society, just as we so classify the murder of a policeman." The newspapers quoted the letter on their front pages and the public was in full agreement.

It was at that meeting, for the first time since his death, that Alex seriously considered telling the police both what she knew and what she suspected. But she eventually dismissed the idea, even felt revulsion at considering such a betrayal. It went against everything she believed about friendship, about loyalty. Would a mother betray the location of a missing son wanted by the police? Would a spouse provide to police information that would result in the incarceration of a husband or wife? Tradition says a resounding no to such a suggestion. How far does that dilemma stretch, to what degree of relationship or friendship? Alex did not know. She never had a reason to pose the question. The first test of her loyalty came near the end of the meeting. "Where is Celia? How could she miss such an important meeting?"

Alex spoke. "I wonder if she's up at her cabin and has not heard the news. She and Jack decided when they bought the place that it would be a real getaway, no TV and no radio." She paused and looked around the table. There was no reaction, so she continued. "After all, it's only been two days since this happened."

The Council president asked a logical question. "But, Alex, surely Jack would have run up there and informed her, or some neighbor would have informed her. I mean, it is her pastor we are talking about." Then, looking at me, he asked, "And why did you not go up there yourself, Alex?"

She was not prepared for the question, but she handled it well. "Oh, I'm sure I should have. But, to be honest, she was the furthest thing on my mind. I went into shock, did not even come out of my house until this meeting tonight. And, let me say again, this only happened two days ago. I'm still paralyzed, barely made it here tonight. Besides, any one of you could have found out where she was and told her. But, you were probably all in the same condition as me."

Her explanation, coming from her only half alert mind, went over very well, especially since it also took them off the hook. "Of course, Alex, we are all in shock. We understand." The air was muggy and close. In the heat of this day, they talked over tall glasses of iced tea, condensation glistening all along their length, like the sweat of lovers in motion. The meeting was adjourned. Alex left with a heavy heart, full of disturbing self-questioning. Where did her duty lie?

The following day they buried Gregory, the man Alex loved. She was determined to be as calm as possible, but that, as it turned out, was not necessary. Everyone cried, men, women and children. They invited the priest in the neighboring parish to say the Mass and preach the homily, but the Archbishop, aware of Gregory's extraordinary reputation and popularity, announced that he would do both. Alex was not so sure Father Gregory would have approved, but then, he tried to reach out to all, including, one can assume, an Archbishop. One of our members commented, when he heard the news, "They tell us to pray for the Archbishop at every Mass. I guess no one needs prayers more than these political ecclesiastics. How do you think they got to the top?"

Father Gregory was also Chaplain to the local police, so they showed up in large numbers. In addition to the Archbishop's sermon, representatives of the police, the firefighters and various civic organizations were given time to make brief remarks of consolation. It was a beautiful ceremony, a fitting tribute to a great man, a man who lived in a clerical world, but never got caught up in clericalism, the bane of true spirituality in the priesthood. Alex recalled his words: "We must never mistake religion for spirituality."

Alex did not want to go to the graveside. Luckily, several others did not want to go either. It was too painful. She simply followed their cars as they drove away. She did not want to see him lowered into the ground. That was not the last image she wanted to have of him. Alex preferred to remember how the strong policemen carried this strong man on their shoulders to the waiting funeral car. That was her last sight of him. From a distance, as they were entering their cars, they heard the Archbishop over the loudspeakers intone the parting words, "Eternal rest grant unto Gregory, O Lord. May his soul and the souls of all the faithful departed, through the mercy of God, rest in peace. Amen" Even pygmies like this archbishop are thrust higher than their true stature when they enunciate the beautiful words of the gospel.

Amen, indeed. He was a man of peace, destroyed by a vengeful woman, who, in spite of her own obscenities, catapulted an imprudent moment on his part into a major disaster. May he rest in well-deserved peace, Amen.

CHAPTER TWENTY SIX

Alex decided not to visit Celia, unless she was invited. She had to watch her closely, and the best way to do that, she concluded, was to let her make all the moves, like tracking an animal in the forest. This way she might better discern where she was going-- what were her intentions. The call came on the weekend following the funeral. "Why don't you come up Friday for a long week-end. I head back Sunday afternoon. That will give us a full couple of days to go over things. There is so much to talk about. I've been speechless. Who could have done such a horrible deed? It's all like a nightmare, isn't it?"

"I will try to come. We're all in shock. It hasn't really sunk in fully yet. I think it's going to be worse later. The entire town is in mourning. There were so many tributes."

Alex noted that, incredibly, she said not a word about the funeral, That would be noticed by a novice. It is customary for women to talk, sometimes too much, about the funeral of a friend. How many showed up? What important personages were there? What did the wife or mother or girlfriend wear? She was not being as clever as she could be. That said something, but what? She had a strategy and Alex needed to figure it out. She interpreted all of this: her going away conveniently so as to be able to say that she was up in the cabin the day of the murder; Jack's failure to call her; his pretence that he did not drive up and tell Celia because he felt she would be too upset; his failure to contact Alex either before the funeral or afterward. One conclusion: He knew she murdered Gregory. Knowing him, in spite of all her infidelities, he would never breathe a word of his suspicions or outright knowledge, to anyone. Perhaps she informed him, knowing he would be suspicious anyway, and begged him to cover for her if necessary. Alex was certain that she planned with him a cover story. She could be ruthlessly meticulous.

In addition, Celia had to assume that Alex suspected, even felt certainty, that she murdered Gregory. Her theory was, in summary, that Celia had neutralized Jack, and the invitation to the cabin was based on her need to neutralize Alex, whatever that took. Sadness and death had sprayed itself over the three of them. Is Celia someone who needed to silence a possible witness? Or, would she believe that Alex would never implicate her? Would she never imagine harming her best friend? Alex didn't know really, but not wanting to do harm and not doing harm are not one and the same thing. The former would depend on the circumstances surrounding the latter. After all, she killed Gregory.

Alex had never desired, until now, to engage in incantation. In fact, she always thought it silly, and part of a primitive culture. Yet, here she was sitting in her living room, paralyzed, unable to engage even herself in meaningful communication, and wanting to repeat something over and over and over, in Veda-like mantra. For next two days Alex spent in mourning; images of his body movements, his smile, his kindness, the way he was with people, replacing all else in her imagination. She could recall and hear his sermons, almost word for word. The delicacy of his preaching art produced a sensuousness that carried his words deep into their souls. After lunch on Friday she packed an overnight bag and headed for the cabin. She had mixed feelings, she even considered the thought that, after all, the two of them had been friends since childhood, and Gregory was now dead. Did Alex not need to live with the living? Could they not put their lives in order with a new beginning, a renewed friendship, each of them having become more profound in their thinking since Gregory? Orderliness becomes us, even in the midst of the arbitrariness that infects our daily living. Ever since Alex had known Celia she had been dishonest, clever, self-serving to an extreme. Of course, that did not prevent her from remaining Celia's friend and confidant over many years, but that was before Gregory.

Her life now is partitioned, before and after Gregory. That is not just a sentimental exaggeration; it is a fact of life. He, with the masculine gentleness that was his hallmark, gave all of them a new view of the world. None of them in this parish will ever be the same, will ever be satisfied with the kind of Christian community that they were accustomed to. Alex would say "masculine" gentleness because strong men have a way of being gentle that is so different from the sort of limping gentleness of lesser men. It is a gentleness so much appreciated by women because there is no obsequiousness to it, nor is it an affectation designed to seduce. It is straightforward and easily recognized as genuine.

The road leading to the cabin wound its way along endless groves of pine trees, from which deer, lightning in their alertness, glanced her way for a mini-second, then leapfrogged across her path. At one turn along the road Alex could see the cabin silhouetted against the bright afternoon sky. She recognized the tiny dot that was Celia as she sat on the cabin porch, dressed in plaid. From that distance she was still, but Alex knew that in that blurb of humanity staring down at here, fire raged. She just knew it. Celia recognized Alex's station wagon from her perch, and waved a white cloth. As Alex pulled up alongside the cabin she stood at the porch railing, her hands firmly set on its crossbar, a thin smile coloring her otherwise pale face. It was clear that she was controlling some form of anxiety mixed with rage. In a slow, sluggish manner she moved to Alex's car and kissed her on the cheek. Sporting a dull musty odor, she obviously had not bathed nor brushed her teeth for the day. As Alex emerged from the car, she took her overnight bag and led her into the cabin. Alex needed to see it, to see where stood her loved one's murderer, smell the stench of her assuaged, unspoken guilt. She knew it would hurt, but she just had to do it.

There was little life in her, a figure of drained limpness. Her greeting was clothed in awkwardness, a greeting that lacked poetry, but not tragedy. Dread ruled Alex as Celia handled her bag. "You know your room. Check it out. I'm not feeling well today. Hope everything you need is there."

Decaying wicker furniture filled the log cabin, together with a queen-size mattress simply tossed on the floor of each bedroom, a barely functioning gas stove and a non-functioning refrigerator. It held musty smells for being closed most of the time. It was dark and gloomy but that would mean nothing in the sparkling heat of a passionate embrace.

Alex entered the room in a haze of hopelessness, aware that their former friendship was torn, tattered, in total disarray. She wanted to bind herself around the trunk of Celia's body like ivy, squeezing and twisting until her last breath expired in her face, where she could see it, smell it, know that it was the last. The thoughts she had on the drive to the cabin about the two of them were starting all over again, showing their absurdity in her demeanor. Reality is sometimes so terribly difficult. Reality has its own timetable; does not always wait for us to catch up. Celia and Alex reuniting? Could it ever be again as it was when Alex quit their private school and then, missing it, returned, with Celia waiting for her, hugging her at the entrance gate? Oh God: how long had she lived in lala-land, pretending against all the evidence that she and Celia were soul mates? What wasted years, what energy misplaced. How awful. That's all over now, but the tenuousness of her rationality had tricked her into thoughts of reconciliation as recently as the hour before, as her car wound its way. How impossible! She had, in fact summoned Alex for her death. She knew it from the moment she heard the news of Gregory's death! How and when will she strike? Has she formulated it neatly, like her engineering drawings, or is she yet playing at her Machiavellian designs, figuring out the best strategy?

Beyond the personal, how did they, in their own separate journeys, get from where each of was, say, fifteen years ago, to where they are now, sitting on the mound of manure that is the pitiful product of their historical actions? What is the answer? There are, of course, no answers. There are no answers because they do not even know the appropriate questions. It's all in God's hands, you see, from alpha to omega. Alex had that thought as she glanced out the window of her room, out toward the edge of the woods, and there it was, a gaping hole, dug out of the black earth. Astride it, a generous supply of soil lay quietly, unaware of its precise function, but sensing its return from whence it came. This time it would not be alone. Alex would be their captain, their companion. There would be respect. The soil would accompany her to her final resting place. Celia must have dug it herself. There was no end to her strength, even in the midst of tragedy, perhaps especially in the midst of tragedy. After all, was not the tragic her natural habitat? Of course it was. But then: how silly to bury a victim at the site of the murder. Alex would have given her much more credit for clear thinking. They would find her. Celia would be accused. Madness had become her mate.

Alex dallied in her room. She did not want to face what was

going to happen, the inevitable. Something in her voice, her body language told Celia that she knew. She waited for her in the other room, perhaps anxiously, Alex was not sure. She knew not only with the natural knowledge of soil heaped aside a gaping hole, but also with intuition. Not woman's intuition, but bedrock humanity intuition. She showered, rubbed my body with oil, assisting the executioner with its burial preparation. Then she sat on the bed, just waiting. Incredibly, she was not nervous.

"What the hell are you doing in there?"

"I'll be out in a few minutes."

"I have something for us to eat. Ready to eat?"

Eat? Who the hell wants to dine with their love's assassin? "Sort of, but let me try a beer first, if you have."

"I have."

"I also brought some sandwiches."

That must have pleased you Celia. Your victim provided food for the post-execution party. The woman who always served you, who always took second place had dared to reach for your prize, so you were duty bound to right the wrong. As you see, dear Celia, you had nothing to fear from Alex. She brought the refreshments. Was that not the ultimate act of service?

"We won't need too much food."

We won't? Why? Oh, of course, silly me, she will lack physical appetite after her appetite is satisfied. That makes sense, really. Good thinking, Celia. You are an admirable piece of work.

When Alex emerged Celia was sitting at the table, simply staring at her silently. She studied Alex's facial expression and her body language. Her eyes surveyed from shoulder to shoulder, from head to toe. She nervously dropped a napkin and suddenly began drumming her fingers on the table where they sat, with neither of them able to speak. It was all out there. She knew Alex knew. Alex knew she knew Alex knew. In that scenario, what was there to chat about? The news? On her lap, barely concealed by a washcloth, the gun sat quietly, ready to obey its mistress.

"How was your drive?"

"Good."

"How long did it take you?"

"About three hours."

"Oh, you must be tired. Look, try the soup. It is freshly

made. Here is your beer. Anything else?"

Alex did not answer and the tension stuck out like clothes in an overstuffed suitcase.

"Are you tired, Alex?"

"Yes, very tired."

"You will soon sleep," she said, with an ironic smile.

Then, like the thrust of a sword, Alex blurted out, "He is dead. He is dead.   My God, Celia, he is dead."

She projected eyes of steel. "A lot of people die every day, and most of those people are ordinary, decent people. We need to mourn for them, not for con artists."

Alex stared with disbelief at her cruelty. "Celia, how can you speak like this. My God, lady, what is wrong with you?"

At this point she remained cool and distant. "My dear Alex, here was a man who flirted with me, made me believe he loved me. I responded, and as soon as I responded he dumped me. I regret his death, of course, but his death does not make him a good man, certainly not a hero. I say that he deserved to die so that he will not philander with other women anymore. His death has liberated me from a house of horrors." She leaned toward Alex and put her lips to her ear. "Aren't you happy for my liberation, dear Alex?" She leaned back and, laughed an evil laugh, drowning me in a torrent of obscenities. The air was dark and foreboding. Self-preservation! Alex lunged at her. They struggled. A shot went off and she fell against the side of the dining room table, propped up by it, the gun still tightly gripped by her fingers. Alex drew back and they locked eyes. She remained quiet as a small rivulet of blood began to find its way down from her midsection. Her eyes continued to focus on Alex's, finally closed, as she entered a world of silence, but not in peace. Alex wished she had garnered a moment of peace. No one should die in such a manner. No one.

The town of Apple Grove was stunned at the news of her 'suicide.' Parishioners were delicate. Not one used the word. "Her passing," was as close as they got in referring to her death. The Parish Council met once again to prepare for yet another funeral. Council members extolled her service as a Eucharistic minister. The pro-tem pastor spoke of the double tragedy that had hit the parish. "How much more can we take?" he asked, as if he felt real emotion in either death. But, Alex understood, it is his duty to pretend, part of the job, part of the ritual.

Alex was asked to speak at the funeral service, along with Celia's husband, Jack. He declined. She gave a brief summary of her relationship with Celia since childhood, and her rise to the very responsible position she held at the Tool and Die Company. Alex found herself imitating the priest. We all act, don't we, when the occasion calls for it?

It was all very proper and traditional. She died with her reputation intact. Jack spread the word that she was very troubled, did not know what she was doing, would never have committed suicide in her right mind. Everyone wanted to believe him, so they did. After the cemetery service, which Jack did attend, he invited Alex to his girlfriend's home for coffee. They sat in almost total but friendly silence. His girlfriend greeted her and then left us space for reminiscing or whatever it is they were to talk about. He was really a broken man; he had given up all sense of self. He said, "I'm lucky Terri loves me and is kind to me. I don't know why she should be, but she is. She took me in like a stray dog." Whatever Jack knew; whatever he surmised about Gregory, Celia, Alex never knew and she would never know. Jack was the soul of discretion, the depositor of secrets. He was fortunate in a way because he did not identify himself as anything or anyone in particular. When he dies it will not be proper to say, "He has passed into oblivion." You see he was the essence of oblivion. Perhaps, in the next world we shall discover that the Jacks of this world, while appearing somewhat useless, mere cumbersome wards of society, are the true inheritors of the Kingdom. Who really knows?

Now, you can read the manner of Gregory's death. It was the very last entry in her diary.

"I did not give him a warning telephone call. For several days I watched his habits. Usually, early evenings he spent with Alex, my betrayer. Sometimes he spent the nights with her. I became a bird watcher by night, devious by day. She stole him from me. I will perform the ultimate ritual. I will send them to lie side by side. Let them try to make love now. I will have the last laugh.

The night of nights began as I tracked him to his office from her home. He was sloppy, leaving the back door unlocked. That was the key, his trustworthiness. It served me well, him ill. He loved his music, and so did I. After all, it enabled me to walk right up to him as he poured over the finance books. I slid the gun aside his cheek and he looked up, his eyes looking straight into the gun's barrel. 'I knew you were coming,' he said, 'I have been waiting for you. I left the door unlocked for days.' He handed me a tiny package. 'I never had the opportunity to lay this at Virginia's grave, so I saved it for you, for you are already dead. You keep it instead.' He opened the package and there lay the pin he purchased in Hyde Park. 'Let me pin it on you to go to the grave with you. Go soon. You are tarrying. Come and meet me.' Then he turned around and picked up his crucifix. 'Now is the time.' I pressed the gun against the right ear. He exploded. That is how it had to end. And now, unhappy as I am, I must plot a strategy to kill my betrayer, so that, one day, in the not too distant future, we three may reunite. I will save one bullet for myself. My birthday is coming soon. It will be the birthday present I give myself, reuniting me with him and her. That's the way it should be. May God bless and keep the three of us. Amen. Celia."

So, my dear, reader, that is the story of Celia, Gregory and Alex. It's not a heroic story, but it is their story. Alex's history ended with them. There will be nothing to say about her after today. She intends to join Jack in his anonymity. She will do her duty. She will return, as soon as the grass grows green over the newly-settled graves and plant flowers for them, dedicating a tiny little garden to their memory. She and Jack are the only ones left to tend to them.

Jack asked Alex to go with him to the cabin the next weekend to clean it up, put in some decent furniture, some photos of Celia, a real carpet on the floor of the dining/living room. He wants to install indirect lighting, to soften the cabin's ambience, for lovers. Jack is going to rent it, selectively and cheaply, to those who really can't afford more expensive places and/or who need to hide their love making. "I will always be able to spot them; I learned from the Queen herself."

He is going to make a plaque for the living room wall, to read, 'May all who use this cabin say a prayer for the woman who built it, Celia Townsend, a good woman. May the good Lord sweep her up in His bosom for all eternity--Amen.'

He used her maiden name. Jack, being who he is, did not consider himself worthy to memorialize her with his name. That is Jack, the only one who escaped unscarred. He is their curator. They needed a man like Jack in their lives. When Alex joins them, she will tell them all the good things Jack is doing. When he dies, all that remains of him will be love; he never really had anything else. But, what a legacy! They will be pleased.

There are a few things Alex must straighten out before she joins them. First of all, she wants to goad the parish council to move ahead with the scholarship memorial they resolved to establish in his honor. People, in the throes of great excitement, or joy or sorrow make wonderful, sometimes even unrealistic pledges. Alex will see to it that this pledge is honored. It will be easy. She has just been elected as chairperson of the parish council. The new priest, a mild, withdrawn personality with a reputation of never stirring the waters, gave his enthusiastic approval. It was his moment to shine among us. He knew that the entire town was enamored of Gregory, loved him, and admired him. This was the new pastor's opportunity to win the approval of everyone, in one fell swoop. Things could never have been better than this. He publicly announced that he would request the parish council to erect a dignified plaque to Gregory's memory in the vestibule, a plaque worthy of the greatness of the man. The entire Congregation stood and clapped and actually cheered. He beamed. He, the man from nowhere, the man the archbishop used only to fill in, whose parishioners, when he left their parish, never missed him. This man had become a legend in his time.

Alex is going to do now what she has often done, pour her a glass of Italian wine, from an Italian vineyard, and toast the greatest Italian she had ever known, the man she loved. *Salute*, (health) dear Gregory, *salute*! AND THEN SHE WILL PUT THE GUN BARREL IN HER MOUTH AND HASTEN HER MEETING WITH CELIA AND GREGORY. IT WAS IN THE STARS THAT THIS WOULD HAPPEN, AND IT DID!

Made in the USA
Charleston, SC
24 May 2011